Confessions of a Gangsta 2

Lock Down Publications & Ca$h
Presents
Confessions of a Gangsta 2
A Novel by *Nicholas Lock*

Confessions of a Gangsta 2

Lock Down Publications
P.O. Box 944
Stockbridge, Ga 30281

Visit our website at www.lockdownpublications.com

Copyright 2020 by Nicholas Lock
Confessions of a Gangsta 2

First Edition November 2020
Printed in the United States of America

This is a work of fiction. Names, characters, places, and incidents either are products of the author's imagination or are used fictitiously. Any similarity to actual events or locales or persons, living or dead, is entirely coincidental.

Cover design and layout by: **Dynasty's Cover Me**
Book interior design by: **Shawn Walker**
Edited by: **Jill Duska**

Stay Connected with Us!

Text **LOCKDOWN** to 22828 to stay up-to-date with new releases, sneak peaks, contests and more…

Submission Guideline

Submit the first three chapters of your completed manuscript to ldpsubmissions@gmail.com, subject line: Your book's title. The manuscript must be in a .doc file and sent as an attachment. Document should be in Times New Roman, double spaced and in size 12 font. Also, provide your synopsis and full contact information. If sending multiple submissions, they must each be in a separate email.

Have a story but no way to send it electronically? You can still submit to LDP/Ca$h Presents. Send in the first three chapters, written or typed, of your completed manuscript to:

LDP: Submissions Dept
Po Box 944
Stockbridge, Ga 30281

*DO NOT send original manuscript. Must be a duplicate. *

Provide your synopsis and a cover letter containing your full contact information.

Thanks for considering LDP and Ca$h Presents.

Nicholas Lock

Shout-outs

Y'all got on me about not shouting nobody out in part 1. This might not be what you expected, but oh well, you asked for this!

First off, I got to thank the man upstairs for blessing me with a crazy imagination and the gift to play with words.

Mama! You already know I love you. You've been the only consistent person on my team through these eleven years. It's almost over now!

My babies, Coco and Aniyah. I love y'all to the moon and back! Coco, you already know what time it is. Stay team Daddy! Aniyah, we ain't talked in a hot minute, but I know it's not your fault so it's all good, because when I come home, we going to make up for all this lost time.

P. C, T-Lee, Lil J, Poppa, Maino, Real. Y'all know what it is. I told y'all I was gonna come shake this urban shit up. I love y'all like brothers and I appreciate all the motivation and the "constructive criticism". I ain't going to say no names... Real.

Sha Loc, you my brother! From the sandbox we been kicking, so you know where we stand. You move, I move, you slide, I slide. All I'z on me!

Murph, Perp, Ross, & TJ, boy do I got some choice words for y'all. Y'all know I love y'all like family. Y'all done ate at my mama's house and vice versa. So tighten up! 2023 I'm trying to shake the world.

6

Tashae, don't be mad at me! Love you, li'l sis. R.I.P. big sister Kentavia Bonner.

Last but not least, I got to shout out Cash and the whole LDP staff for giving me a shot and making all this possible.

To all the haters and naysayers, keep doing what you doing. I'm just gon' go harder!

FAYETTEVILLE! We here now! Y'all know I'm about to put on for the city! AANNANT!

To anybody I forgot, my bad, I got you next time.

Nick Lock

Nicholas Lock

Chapter 1

Ooh shit! This definitely was not going to turn out good. If Ms. Kiana killed Isabella's mom, then nine times out of ten, the only thing that was going to appease Hector was somebody in OTF's head. All Taz knew was that it wasn't going to be Kiki's!

"Your mom killed my mom! I knew it was a reason I didn't like your ass!" Isabella yelled as she tried to get to Kiki.

"Bella, sit your ass down! Now is not the time!" Taz stopped her before she could get in range of Kiki.

"Taz, you remember when we first started doing business and I told you that your enemies are my enemies and my enemies are your enemies? Well, OTF is one of my main enemies. So you're either with me or against me," Hector told Taz.

"First off, that was while we were doing business together. You know I'm no longer involved with that. Now as far as you doing something to someone in OTF, I have no say. But doing harm to Kiki is a deal breaker," Taz said as he cocked his hammer.

"Do you understand what you're saying?" Hector asked, not flinching.

"Like I told you before, this isn't Meosha, nor is she a part of OTF. True indeed, Ms. Kiana is her mother, but this is her first time meeting her since she was a baby."

"So you have no loyalty to OTF?" Hector asked Kiki with a raised brow.

"My loyalty is to Taz, but OTF is still my blood," Kiki spoke up for the first time.

"Daddy, can we have something to drink?" His daughters burst into the living room.

"Go back to y'all's room until I get done," he said and Isabella ushered them out of the room.

"You know what, Kiki? I have an ultimatum for you," Hector told her, clasping his hands behind his back. "You can either assist me in avenging my wife's death, or you can be a part of the death toll. It makes no difference to me. I don't want an answer now. I'll give you a few days to mull it over," he said and then walked out with his goons in tow.

When he walked out, Taz looked at Kiki because he knew she most likely already had her mind made up and he had a pretty good idea what her decision was going to be. Before Kiki had a chance to say anything, Isabella walked back in the room and started blanking.

"Bitch, get the fuck out my house! Now!" she yelled.

"Bella, I swear to God! Stay the fuck out of this," Taz told her.

"Stay out of it? Her mom killed my mother and you say stay out of it? No, fuck that!" she spat.

"You know what? I'm sick of this shit! You want smoke with Kiki? Go ahead then and tell me how it works out for your seven month pregnant ass," he said and then walked out to get his babies something to drink.

As soon as Taz left the room, Isabella rushed Kiki. Kiki sidestepped her, pushed her on the couch, and got on top of her.

"What's your fucking problem? Are you suicidal? I know you know I'll kill your ass," Kiki told Isabella.

"And I'll kill you!" Bella said, trying to push Kiki off her.

Kiki slapped Bella and put her gun under her chin. "If you weren't pregnant with my brother's baby, I'd decorate the living room with your brains. I know what your bird-ass problem really is too. You're jealous of the relationship me and Taz got. But I got a newsflash for you. I was here before you and I'm going to be here long after you! Keep this in mind, little girl: if I wanted Taz, I'd have him! Get your shit together,

10

little girl. Make this your last time trying me until you have his baby. Then I'm going to give you what you want!"

"Let her up," Taz said, leaning up against the wall. "I hope y'all got that little girl shit out your system." He looked at them both. "Kiki, what are you going to do?"

"Taz, stop playing with me, you already know what time it is," she said, solidifying what he thought.

"Bella, what are you going to do?"

"Are you asking me if I'm going to go against my father?" she asked with her brow raised. Taz just looked at her. Isabella copied Kiki and said, "Taz, stop playing with me, you already know what time it is," and then walked out of the room, leaving him wondering.

Taz knew what Kiki meant when she said Hector had better beef his security up, but with Isabella, he honestly didn't know what she meant. Taz knew when it came to him, Isabella would move a mountain, but if it required her to go against her pops, he really couldn't say. But time would tell. He wasn't going to stress himself trying to figure it out. One thing he did know: Isabella wouldn't do him any bodily harm - at least, he didn't think so.

***

Taz was on the next flight out to Atlanta to see what was so important that TK wanted to talk to him in person.

"Oh, you doing it like that?" Taz asked as TK pulled up to pick him up from the airport in the new Maserati Gran Turismo on 22's.

"This ain't shit! Wait until you see what PJ riding in."

"I can only imagine. But what was so urgent that you had me come all the way up here?"

"Man, the last time I talked to Juan, he told me that I was going to have to stop dealing with OTF. And he told me that I needed to get my soldiers ready because the cartel was about to wipe OTF off the map and we was going to help him," TK told Taz.

"I knew that's what this was about," Taz said, taking a deep breath and leaning his seat back.

"So you already knew about this and you ain't tell us?"

"I just found out yesterday. Hector ran in my house trying to snatch Kiki up, talking about she's Meosha, but you know that wasn't about nothing."

"And how Kiki react?" TK already knew there was a story to be told.

"Check it. He told Kiki that she could either help him take OTF down or be a part of the death toll."

"Oh man, he tripping."

"He told her he was going to give her a minute to make her mind up, but you know her mind was made up before he left. So this how it's going to go down. I do need you to get your soldiers ready and I want you to holler at Juan and re-up, but you need to get triple of what y'all been getting. Because when they find out we not going against OTF, they going to cut y'all off and come for y'all's head. So get that work and switch all the spots up. Drop me off at Ms. Kiana's investigation firm."

The rest of the ride was quiet, each of them in their thoughts. Taz was trying to figure out how he was going to ensure his niggas got through this whole ordeal unscathed. The more he thought about it, the more he realized there was a good chance that wasn't about to happen. Hector and his cartel were a hundred times worse than the Zoe Pound and they had way more power and resources, but Taz kept an ace in the hole.

While Taz was thinking about his issues, TK was thinking about how much money they were going to be missing by cutting Juan off. He knew plugs like the Mexican cartel only came around once in a lifetime and here they were getting ready to walk away from one willingly. Not to mention the work was top notch. He just hoped it all worked out.

"Are you going to need a ride when you leave here?" TK asked as they pulled up outside the investigation firm.

"Nah, I'm good," Taz told him. He gave him some dap and got out.

Once inside the building, Taz got on the elevator and rode it to the top floor. The first thing he saw when he got off the elevator was a big gold sign that said Supreme Investigations. He walked to the reception desk and asked if Ms. Kiana was in

"She's in a meeting right now. Do you have an appointment?" the secretary asked.

"What about Meosha?" Taz asked, ignoring her question.

"You're going to have to make an appointment," she said curtly.

"What? You better call. Better yet, I know what to do," he said as he started walking down the hallway.

"You can't go back there! I'm calling security!" she yelled towards his back.

Taz walked down the hall, trying to find Kiki's mom's office. He turned down another hallway and heard a bunch of footsteps behind him. He turned around to see four security guards and the secretary coming his way.

"That's him right there!" she pointed.

"You need to come with us," one security guard said aggressively.

"Go find you something safe to do." Taz smiled and turned to walk off.

One of the security guards took Taz's smile the wrong way and grabbed his shoulder as he was walking down the hallway. Taz turned, pushed him against the wall, and put his fire under his chin.

"Didn't I tell you to find something safe to do?"

"Let him go, Taz," Ms. Kiana said from behind him.

He turned to see her and Meosha walking his way. They were both dressed in business suits. The only real difference was that Meosha's skirt was shorter.

"Taz, go with Meosha. I'll handle this."

Taz put his gun up and followed Meosha. She led him down another hallway to her office.

"You need to calm your ass down," she said once they were in the office.

"Who you think you talking to?" Taz narrowed his eyes.

"You, duh!" She sat on the edge of her desk, making her skirt ride up higher.

Instead of responding, he just took her in. It was amazing to him how much alike she and Keosha looked. He'd never been around identical twins before. The only way you could tell them apart was their voices and their personalities.

"So what brings you to Atlanta?"

"I got to holler at your moms," he said, looking around her office.

"I thought you was coming to see me," she stated, causing him to look back her way.

"Meosha, go ahead with that shit." He looked her in the eyes.

"If you find Kiki attractive, it's no way you don't think I'm sexy." She opened her legs, showing off some pink lace panties, which looked damn good against her pitch black skin.

"Meosha, Kiki'll fuck you up, stop playing." He stood up and got ready to walk out.

14

"Anyways." She got up and got in front of him. "Y'all already said y'all not girlfriend and boyfriend, so what's the problem?" She put her breasts on his chest.

As he got ready to say something, Ms. Kiana walked in and Meosha jumped back. She looked back and forth from Meosha to Taz, raised one of her brows, and then sat down behind Meosha's desk.

"So to what do I owe this visit?" OTF's matriarch questioned.

"Look, the Mexican Cartel has OTF in its crosshairs. Hector said you killed his wife. He gave Kiki an ultimatum to either help him take OTF down or die. So it's a war on the horizon," he informed her.

"How do you even know Hector's bitch ass?" she wanted to know.

"He's my plug, plus his daughter is about to have my baby."

"Interesting," Ms. Kiana said with a smirk.

"And what is your role going to be when the shit hits the fan?" Meosha asked.

"Anybody that tries to spill Kiki's blood is going to be on a first class flight to meet their maker," Taz said before walking out the door.

Nicholas Lock

Chapter 2

"Where you at?" Quanesha asked Taz

"Damn, I don't get no 'Hey, I missed you' or nothing, huh?"

"Bae, you already know all that. I'm just trying to figure out why you ain't called me," she said in her heavily-accented voice.

"I'm in Atlanta, but I'll be back in Miami in a few days after I wrap some shit up."

Ever since Quanesha had transferred from Fayetteville State University to the University of Miami, they had been fucking like rabbits. What Taz loved most was that she knew he had a lady and wasn't tripping. Taz had the best of both worlds. He had a bad bitch at home and a super bad bitch on the side. On the low, Taz had a thing for Nesha's high yellow ass. He didn't know what it was, but she had her claws in him. If he would've met her before Bella, he might have wifed her up. His only problem was that she was only nineteen. But there was no way for you to know she was that young unless she told you. She was a true stallion at 5'11" and 220 pounds, but her stomach was nonexistent. All that weight was in her breasts and lower body. She had to have a fifty-inch ass and it had a mind of its own the way it moved. Then with her being from Barbados, she had a heavy island accent. Everything about her was exotic. Taz always told her she had to be half-Asian because her eyes were so chinky. Then her fire red dreads that fell past her ass were the icing on the cake.

"So as soon as you come back, we gon' chill, right?"

"Yeah, bae, I got you. Now can I go handle my business?"

"Bye, boy."

Taz was on the way to a meeting with his boys. There was some conflict going on about the decision to cut Juan off and even though Taz had fallen back from the game and left TK in charge, they still respected his mind. He was just going to try to explain to them why it would be wise to go ahead and get as much work as possible and be done with it. They were meeting at a hookah bar and lounge in downtown Atlanta. Taz had never been to a hookah bar before so he didn't know what to expect.

A cloud of smoke hit him in the face as soon as he opened the door, but it wasn't a bad smoke. It had a fruity smell to it. It was nothing like he expected. When his eyes adjusted, he saw TK, Reggie, and PJ sitting at a table in the very back. He gave his niggas some dap and sat down where he could see the door.

"Now what's the issue?" Taz asked.

"Bro, I'm not feeling this whole cut the plug off shit. Why would we do that? Do you know how much money we going to be losing? That's our bread and meat. You straight. You got the whole legit thing going," PJ spoke his feelings.

"And whose fucking fault is that? I told you motherfuckers to get y'all shit together and get some legit shit going, but y'all want to be dope boys forever!" Taz said, getting heated.

"If we do cut him off, what we going to do about work once we run out?" Reggie questioned.

After hearing the question, Taz leaned back in his chair and took a good look at his boys. Was this the beginning of the end? Because it was looking like they were questioning him in ways that they never had.

"Yo, check it out. Haven't I always come through in the clutch? And before you answer that, answer this. What you mean *if* y'all cut him off? Ohhh... So y'all not dead set on cutting Juan off, huh?" Taz started smiling "So what, y'all plan on going against OTF? Huh?" He didn't get a response, and that sent his temper through the roof. "Ha, ha, ha, y'all niggas got shit fucked up! Y'all act like I'm going to leave y'all niggas on stuck! I'm the reason the plug even fucking with y'all - or did y'all forget that? I know something else you niggas forgot and I don't understand how. What y'all going to do about Kiki?" He leaned back and clasped his hands behind his head.

They all looked at each other because they knew Kiki would rain down hell on them. They couldn't fuck with Kiki when it came to blowing smoke. It was going to be in their best interest to get their minds right because she wasn't going to let anybody harm her family.

"Damn, why ain't nobody tell me it was a meeting going down?" Kiki walked up, catching everyone off guard. "What I miss?" she asked, looking around the table. Then her eyes settled on Taz.

"So who going to tell her?" Taz instigated.

"Tell me what?"

"Well, since a cat has y'all's tongues all of a sudden, I'll tell her. They're thinking about siding with the Mexican Cartel over OTF."

"Oh yeah?" she asked, cocking her head to the side.

"Hold up, hold up, we ain't made no decision yet. We just trying to figure out if it's a way around cutting them off. I did what Taz said though and tripled our usual re-up, so we straight in that aspect for a while," TK said, trying to ease some of the tension.

"I ain't tripping. I hope y'all make y'all's mind up quick, and hopefully it's the right decision," Kiki said casually as she sat down beside Taz. "Now if y'all don't mind, I got some shit I need to holler at Taz about."

"That's cool. We need to get to this money anyway," PJ said as they all got up.

"We going to meet up later on tonight," Reggie said.

"Just tell me where," Taz said as they left. "Now what you got to holler at me about, and why was you so calm just now? What you got up your sleeve?"

"I told Hector's bitch ass he can't run from no head shot. I'm not worried about TK and them and their decision, because the cartel going to be gunning for them too. So their decision has already been made. They just don't know it yet," she told Taz.

As Taz was getting ready to respond, they heard shots going off outside. Kiki and Taz rushed outside to make sure TK, Reggie, and PJ were good. When they stepped outside, it was a war zone. TK was pinned down behind his Maserati by some Mexicans in a red Tahoe and Reggie and PJ were ducked down behind PJ's Rolls Royce Phantom coupe, trading shots with another group of Mexicans. Taz and Kiki immediately went into go mode. Taz went left and Kiki went right. He put one in the head of his Glock 21 and went to work. By the time the esse's that were shooting at TK realized he had some help, it was too late. Taz was already up on them. He dropped the driver with a headshot and then the other ones in the Tahoe turned their guns on him, forcing him to dive behind an F-150.

In the process of gunning for Taz, they forgot about TK. He popped up from behind his Maserati, shooting a carbon 15. The rounds from the carbon pierced the Tahoe as if it was paper, hitting everyone inside. With them taken care of, Taz went to try and assist Kiki with the other group of esse's, but when he looked, he saw Kiki, Reggie, and PJ walking their way.

"Y'all good?" they asked when they walked up.

"We is now," replied TK

"Who the fuck was that?" Reggie asked.

"Are you serious?" Taz asked, amazed that he was in denial. "I guess you didn't notice that all them niggas was Mexicans."

"Yeah, bro, those are Juan's people," TK said.

"Guess we ain't got to worry about y'all's decision now. The cartel made it for y'all." Kiki laughed and walked away.

Nicholas Lock

Chapter 3

After the shootout in Atlanta, Taz flew back to Miami because he knew Atlanta was about to be a bloodbath and he wasn't trying to get in the mix - at least, not yet. Then he still had Isabella's pregnant ass to worry about. When it was war time, nobody was safe, and Taz wasn't going to allow her and his son to be a casualty of war. Since he had told Ms. Kiana that Bella was about to have his child, he didn't think OTF would try anything funny, but it was better to be safe than sorry.

The house was quiet when he walked in. He went upstairs and checked on his daughters first. He looked in D'Azia's room and saw her asleep under her Winnie the Pooh covers. Taz walked over and pulled her covers up to her chin. He kissed her on the cheek then made his way to Neveah's room. As expected, she was still up watching cartoons.

"What you still doing up, Princess?"

"Watching Spongebob," she said innocently.

"It's three in the morning. You need to be in the bed. Come on." He pulled the covers back on the bed.

To his surprise, she complied, which let him know she was sleepy. Otherwise, she'd be trying to convince him to let her stay up. He tucked her in and watched her sleep. It had been a while since he'd spent some quality time with his babies. He was slipping. The whole eight years he was in prison he told himself he wasn't ever going to risk going back to prison, but here he was throwing bricks at the penitentiary. After this shit was over, he was going to sit Kiki down and have a long talk. Either she was going to sit her ass down and get this legit money and leave the streets alone, or he was going to cut her off.

After watching Neveah sleep for a while, he got up and made his way downstairs to his bedroom. When he walked in,

Isabella was asleep on top of the covers with one of his wife beaters on. Taz stood at the edge of the bed looking down at her. She looked sexy as fuck sprawled out across the bed with her hair fanned out. After the doctors had shaved the side of her head from Gutta's bullet grazing her, it had grown back and was once again all the way down her back. Taz stripped out of his clothes and started to rub on her butt, causing her to roll onto her side and look at him.

"I heard about Atlanta too," Isabella said as Taz caressed her swollen stomach.

"I'm not trying to talk about that," he said, moving his hand lower.

"Well I am." She grabbed his hand. "You're going to put me in a bad spot. My dad isn't going to care that I'm about to have your baby. Mmm," she moaned as Taz slipped his finger into her already wet pussy.

"Fuck all that, give daddy some of this cat," he said, climbing between her legs.

"Fuck!" she yelled as Taz plunged into her wetness.

"Nah, where you going?" Taz asked as she started trying to run from the dick.

"You know you can't do me like that, papi," she whined. "Let me ride it."

Ever since Bella was about four months along, she wasn't able to take no dick. Taz rolled onto his back as Bella took the wife beater off and climbed onto his lap. She placed her hand on his stomach as she lowered herself onto his dick.

"Taz," she moaned as Taz grabbed her hips, making her rock back and forth.

Taz leaned up and sucked on one of her breasts, causing some breast milk to squirt into his mouth.

"Suck my titties, baby!" she moaned, cradling the back of his head.

"Fuck this," Taz said as he grabbed her hips and lifted her up, carrying her to the dresser

"Nooo, baby!" Bella already knew what time it was.

Taz started slamming into her with deep strokes. Her pussy was so wet that every time he pulled out of her, juices would spill out onto the dresser. "Take this dick, Bella," he said, picking up his pace.

"Papi! Fuck your pussy!" she screamed.

Taz continued to pound away as Isabella moaned his name in his ear. It had been about two weeks since he'd had sex, so he was in a rush to get his nut off.

"I'm about to nut, Bella," he said before releasing his seeds deep inside of her.

"Ugh, you make me sick," she said, climbing down and going into the bathroom to clean up.

While she did that, Taz went and hopped in the bed and before he knew it, he had dozed off. Just as he was getting into a good sleep, Bella came and got in the bed and shook him awake.

"Uh-uh, you not going to sleep." She crawled on top of him

"Go ahead now, Bella." He pulled the covers over his head.

"No, we need to talk." She snatched the covers back.

"Man, damn, girl, what's up?" He opened his eyes

"Like I told you earlier, my daddy is not going to care about me getting ready to have your baby. He'll still have you killed."

"I hope you don't think I'm scared of your punk-ass daddy," Taz stated, fully waking up.

"I know you not, papi, but that still don't mean he won't kill you and I need you here." She started to cry.

"And what are you going to do? Are you going to let him, or is you going to help me?"

"Help you what? Kill my fucking daddy? No! If you weren't stuck at the hip with Kiki's bitch ass, you wouldn't even be in this shit!

"First off, Kiki is my… I'm trying to figure out how I can put this in a way you can understand. I'm just going to give you the short version of how we met. I was robbing a nigga in Atlanta and when I ran in, he had Kiki on her knees jacking him off. She was only sixteen and on top of that, she was his niece, and he'd been molesting her for years. I killed him and brought her back to Fayetteville with me. That's why our bond is so strong."

"Well, you need to tell her to lay low until my father takes care of OTF."

"I don't think it's going to play out the way you think. The family isn't going to be a pushover. And let's say the Mexican Cartel does knock OTF off. Do you think he's going to let Kiki live?" he asked and she got quiet, letting him know everything he needed to know. "Exactly. So you need to find out what role you're going to play in all this," Taz said before rolling over to get some rest.

***

"I thought I was going to have to hunt you down," Quane-sha said as Taz walked into her apartment.

"Yeah, right. You know I was going to come check on my PYT," he replied, making her grin

"Tell me anything," said Quanesha, walking into the kitchen.

Taz couldn't help but stare. Every time she moved, her ass would jiggle uncontrollably, and the purple lace boy shorts had her ass sitting up just right. Taz walked behind her, grabbed both her ass cheeks, pulled them apart, and put his semi-hard dick between them.

"Stop being nasty." She turned around and put his dick back in his pants. "Come on so I can do that nappy head."

Taz followed her down the hallway into her bedroom and sat down on the floor. Nesha grabbed the lock and twist hair grease and a comb and sat down on the edge of the bed.

"Are you going to behave this time?" asked Nesha.

The last time she tried to do his hair, she ended up with her face in the pillow while Taz tried to knock her walls down.

"Yeah. I got some business meetings coming up so my hair needs to be done," he assured her.

"So what we doing today?" she asked, parting his hair.

"You talking about after I mark my territory"

"There you go being nasty again. I want to go to the beach," she stated.

"Well, hurry up and do my hair and we can go."

"You can't rush perfection." She yanked his head back and kissed him.

It didn't take her long to finish his hair. Before he knew it, she was done. She lifted her legs up to let Taz get up and he caught her legs and got eye level with her love box.

"Nooo, baby."

Taz ignored her and sucked her clit into his mouth through her boy shorts. "Take them off," he commanded, taking his Gucci wife beater off.

"Baaabyyy!" she started to whine

She pulled her boy shorts off while at the same time poking her lips out to pout. Taz dived right in, wiping the pout right off her face.

"Yesss," she moaned, wrapping her legs around his neck

Taz started circling her clit with his tongue, making her grab two handfuls of his hair. He started moving two fingers in and out of her center as she writhed around from the assault Taz's tongue was doing on her clit.

"What are you doing?" Nesha whispered.

Taz kept devouring her box as if it was his last meal on earth.

"Make me cum, baby, make me cum."

Taz began flicking his tongue from side to side across her clit and she really lost it.

"Here I cum, baby! Don't stop!" she yelled.

And that's exactly what Taz did. He stopped.

"What are you doing?" she asked as he stood up and walked out of the room. "Are you serious?" She stormed down the hallway after him

"You ready to hit the beach?" asked Taz, sitting down on the couch.

Nesha stood there looking at him like he was crazy, then she ran and hopped on Taz, catching him off guard

"Quit playing, girl." He laughed

She got him on his back and climbed up his body until her pussy was in his face. Taz would've been able to just push the average chick off, but Nesha was almost six feet tall and 220 pounds, so he just let her have her way. He let her ride his face until she drenched his face with her juices.

"You know that was rape, right?"

"Boy, boo." She walked into the back to get dressed.

After she came out, they went to the beach and relaxed. Taz enjoyed the moment because he knew in the coming weeks, his life was going to be anything but normal.

Chapter 4

Taz's businesses were doing well. Weiner Works and Primo's Pizza had made the transition perfectly and they were already turning over profits. Then he'd gotten so good at flipping houses that he'd started his own real estate company called Majestic Realtors and he'd made Mary and Keishana partners in the business. He told them he was going to have a spot for them and he'd come through. He felt like he owed Keishana because she'd risked her life to come to Miami and give the head of the Zoe Pound Mafia AIDS, and she did it with no questions asked. Making them his partners was turning out to be his smartest move yet because nothing made a man spend money faster than a pretty face and a fat ass. They were selling houses faster than bottled water in hell.

Taz was going to be in some important business meetings most of the day, so he'd made sure to dress accordingly. He was wearing a pair of tailored black Tom Ford slacks, a black Tom Ford dress shirt, and some black Prada shoes. The only jewelry he wore was the rose gold Daytona Rolex. His first meeting of the day was with Victoria about Weiner Works. She was supposed to come to Miami just to get the business up and running, but she loved Miami and its weather so much that she decided to stay permanently. Ever since they'd had that one night stand, they'd been super cool. On the low, Taz wanted to hit it again, but he wasn't going to be the one to initiate it.

"How you doing, Mr. Walker?" Victoria asked when Taz walked in.

"I'm good, Vicky, how is everything?"

"Very good, actually. You know, my mom is retiring, so you know your percentage of the company is going to go up. I know we agreed on you getting fifteen percent, but your ideas have made us so much more profitable that we've decided to up that to twenty-six percent," she said.

"That's what I'm talking about!" Taz said, already calculating the numbers in his head

"I knew you'd be happy to hear that, but other than that, everything is the same. Oh! Me and my husband are finally getting a divorce. I'm tired of the physical abuse."

"That's what's up. I'm happy for you," he stated, giving her a hug.

When he tried to break away, she held him and looked up at him.

Taz just looked at her as she stood on her tip toes and kissed him.

"Thanks for being there for me this whole time," Victoria said, finally breaking away.

"You good."

"After my divorce, I want you to throw me a celebration party." She smiled.

Taz laughed while looking her over. She was the first white girl he'd ever fucked in his life. At forty-one, she still looked damn good, and the Miami sun had her tanned just right. The red hair and green eyes made her all the more exclusive. That red hair was probably why Quanesha appealed to him so much.

"Let me know when the divorce is official and I got you," Taz said, ending their meeting

His next meeting was with Johnny, Mr. Tessatore's son. When Taz had come to Mr. Tessatore about expanding his business to Miami, he was immediately on board, but he wanted his son to get his feet wet in the family business. At first Taz was skeptical, but after working with him the last few months, he had Taz's stamp of approval. He was Taz's age at twenty-nine, so they were actually real cool. He was always telling Taz that he needed to try some Italian pussy and Taz always told him how crazy he was.

"What's good, Johnny?"

"My man Taz! How's it going?"

"I can't call it. You know me, just slow motion."

"I wanted to meet with you and ask you what you thought about opening up a second Primo's Pizza down here. I already asked my dad and he said it was up to you."

This was a no-brainer. With a thirty percent stake in the business, Taz was with opening ten more stores.

"Hell yeah, let's do it."

They went over ideas of when and where to open it. Their meeting didn't last an hour. Initially, Taz thought he was going to be in meetings most of the day, but here he was already down two with only one more to go. He was about to meet with Keishana and Mary. This wasn't going to be so much of a business meeting, but rather a get together of friends. He and Mary still fucked from time to time, but it was nothing serious. And Keishana was his road dog.

When he pulled up to the real estate office, Keishana was just getting out of her S550. It was amazing to him how beautiful she still was. Her pitch black skin was still blemish free and she was thick to death. If you put her and Buffie the Body beside each other, you'd mistake them for twins. He respected her to the utmost because when he first came home, he tried to fuck her, but she kept it one thousand with him and told him she had AIDS. She smiled when she saw him staring at her.

"Hey, big daddy," she said, walking up to his car.

He got out of the Ferrari and grabbed her briefcase for her as they were about to go inside the building. Taz realized he'd left his phone in his car.

"Hold up real quick."

He made his way to his car and got his phone and was making his way back to where Keishana was when she said, "Oh my God, Taz!"

He saw the expression on her face and he knew he was more than likely a dead man. When he turned around to see what she saw, he knew it over. There was a group of esse's leaning out the window of two Suburbans wielding assault rifles. Of all the days not to be strapped, he chose today. At least he knew his babies were going to be straight. He smiled, threw his arms out wide, and said, "Do you, pussy, Kiki going to come see about you."

TAT! TAT! TAT! TAT! TAT! They started letting off.

"Noooo!" Keishana yelled as a round from one of the choppas hit him in the chest, knocking him to his back.

He looked up and saw Keishana standing over him crying, and then his vision blacked out.

Chapter 5

"We're gathered here today to bury a father, a brother, a friend, an all-around good person. Brother D'angelo came home from prison and got his life back on track. He turned his life around from an armed robber to an accomplished and successful businessman. He was called home at the young age of twenty-nine," the preacher said.

The funeral was deep! The church was so packed there were people standing up along the walls all throughout the church.

"This is all your fault, bitch!" Isabella yelled in Kiki's direction. "It's supposed to be you, not him!" she continued to scream.

Kiki just stared at her through red, puffy eyes. Taz was the only reason Isabella had lived so long, but as soon as she had his baby, she was dead, Kiki told herself. She was going to raise his son herself. Then she was going to cut Hector's head off and put it on a spike.

BOOM!

The doors of the church busted open and in walked Quanesha in an all-white Chanel pantsuit and some white Chanel flats.

"This is about to get real interesting," Kiki told PJ, TK, and Reggie.

Kiki was the only one who knew who she was. Everyone watched as Quanesha made her way down the aisle towards Taz's casket.

"Bitch, who the fuck are you?" Isabella stood in the way of Quanesha getting to Taz's casket.

Quanesha slapped Isabella to the floor and walked around her to Taz's casket.

"Damn, bae. How you let them suckers catch you slipping?" she asked as a tear slipped down her face. "I need you, Taz. How you going to leave me and I'm pregnant with your child?" she dropped a bombshell.

"Clear!" the EMT said as he placed the defibrillator on Taz's chest, sending on electric shock through his body. "Still no pulse! Clear!" He tried again.

"Oh my God, please help him" Keishana cried, watching the scene play out in the back of the ambulance.

"Got a pulse! Step on it!" the EMT told the driver.

When they got to the hospital, there was a crew waiting on them.

"Twenty-nine-year-old black male with a single gunshot wound to the chest, blood pressure is low! Get him to the OR stat!"

As they wheeled Taz into the back, Mary walked into the emergency room.

"What happened?" she asked Keishana.

"These Mexicans pulled up outside the building and Taz said something to them and they started shooting."

"We got to call TK, PJ, and Reggie," Mary said.

"I got his phone right here," Keishana said and then his phone started to ring. "Oh shit," she said, looking at the screen.

"Who is it?" Mary asked

"Kiki."

They both knew how Kiki was when it came to Taz and neither one wanted to be the one to tell her he was fighting for his life.

"Hello?" Keishana answered.

"Who this?"

"This Keishana, Kiki. Taz got shot by some Mexicans and now we at the hospital. They took him to the operating room as soon as we got here because they had to bring him back while we were in the ambulance." She went ahead and told Kiki everything she needed to know

"What hospital you at?" Kiki whispered.

Keishana hung up after letting Kiki know where they were.

"Girl, Kiki about to bring death and mayhem to some-body's door," Mary said, knowing the consequences that shooting Taz was going to bring.

"God forbid if he don't make it," Keishana added

"Is Mr. Walker's family here?" a doctor asked, stepping into the ER waiting room.

"Yes," Mary and Keishana said in unison

"Let me ease your mind. He's going to make it, but he's lost a substantial amount of blood. We're going to need to run some more tests to make sure there's no internal bleeding. He's in ICU as of right now because of the seriousness of his injury."

"So he's definitely going to live?" Keishana asked

"Barring any unforeseen complications, yes."

"When can we see him?" asked Mary

"Come on." The doctor led them to ICU.

When they walked into Taz's room, they both gasped. Taz had tubes running all through him. They had never seen him look so frail and vulnerable. They were used to the vibrant Taz. Keishana grabbed his hand and squeezed it.

"We told Kiki, and she's on the way. I'm sure she told everyone else. I know you, Taz. Don't be trying to rush back to them streets. Take your time and rest up. Me and Mary can hold the fort down until you get back on your feet," Keishana said

One thing they knew for a fact was that whoever was re-sponsible for him being laid up in the hospital was in for a reality check. They knew Taz before he went away to prison when he was a whole live fool. There was a reason he was called the Tasmanian Devil. He tore up everything in his path. Since coming home, he'd been a new man. He was real laid back. But they'd bet their bottom dollar that when he got back on his feet, the old Taz would be back.

Mary left to go home, but Keishana was going to stay until Kiki or someone else came to the hospital.

***

"Keishana! Keishana!"

"Huh?" Keishana awoke to Kiki yelling her name. She looked around and saw Taz still in the hospital bed. She was hoping yesterday was a bad dream.

"You can go home. I'm here," Kiki told her

Keishana looked Kiki over. She could tell Taz's condition was affecting her.

"Kiki, why you got that trenchcoat on in this hot-ass weather, girl?"

Kiki opened the trenchcoat and Keishana shook her head. Not only did she have a bulletproof vest on, but she had two guns in shoulder holsters and a big-ass rifle on her side. She was ready to go to war.

BEEP! BEEP! BEEP! Taz's heart monitor sped up, causing them to look his way and see that his eyes were open.

"Nigga, you need to get your soft ass up," Kiki stated, making him grin. "Go get the nurse, girl," she said to Keishana.

Kiki helped Taz sit up in his bed.

"I'm leaving," Taz said, barely above a whisper. He was real weak.

"Nah, you're going to rest up, then we're going to make it real bloody fo' the Mexican Cartel. TK, PJ, and Reggie should be here later on and I told your old lady she was on borrowed time."

Keishana slammed the door, causing Kiki to spin around with her fire in her hand. Before Kiki could ask what was going on, Keishana said, "I was at the nurse's station and I seen some Mexicans get off the elevator and start going room to room."

"Fuck!" Kiki grabbed the M4 and cocked it. "You know how to use a gun?"

Keishana nodded her head and Kiki tossed her a .45. "Now help me with Taz."

"Aaahh!" Taz said as they pulled his tubes out.

They put him in a wheelchair and Kiki pulled the bullet-proof vest off. She and Keishana worked it onto Taz. Kiki knew she had to get him out of there. The cartel was out to make a statement and killing Taz, the brains of the crew, would make a hell of a statement.

"Give me a hammer," Taz whispered

"Say what?" Kiki asked

"Give. Me. A. Hammer," he said weakly.

She handed him her other .45 immediately because she remembered how he acted the last time he told her to give him a gun and she didn't.

"Listen, girl, make sure you get him to the elevator and out of here. I don't care if I'm there or not. Come on."

They rushed out the room and ran right into one of the esse's. Kiki let the M4 talk one time. He dropped and they rushed by him as two more came out of another room. Kiki let off, but one of them managed to get two shots off, hitting Taz square in the chest, knocking him unconscious.

"Aaahh! Kiki screamed when she saw Taz slump over. "Check him!" she yelled.

"He good. It didn't go through the vest." Keishana checked Taz

Kiki let off some more shots as another group of esse's came down the hallway, making them duck in different rooms

"GO! GO! GO!" Kiki yelled as she continued to shoot.

Keishana got Taz to the elevator in one piece. She looked down at an unconscious Taz as she waited on Kiki to come. She heard shots continuing to go off. She didn't want to leave Kiki by herself, but she needed to get Taz out of there. She put the wheelchair in the elevator door so it wouldn't close and went to get Kiki. When Keishana peeked around the corner, she saw nurses running around, trying to dodge hot balls that were being sent out of the barrels of the assault rifles.

Then she saw that the Mexicans had Kiki pinned down behind the nurse's station. A doctor was running around, desperate to avoid death. But he ended up running dead smack into it as he darted pass the area where the Mexicans were gunning for Kiki. A barrage of bullets tore him in half.

The Mexicans had their backs to Keishana. Taking full advantage of the opportunity, she pointed her weapon at them and started firing, giving Kiki the chance she needed. Kiki rose up, firing the M4. The ones Keishana didn't hit, Kiki did. They ran off to get Taz out of the hospital. They got him to the rental and swerved off.

"Oh my God! He's bleeding bad," Keishana said from the backseat.

"Ma, I need you to call some of your people! They tried to kill Taz at the hospital and he's bleeding real bad," Kiki said, swerving in and out of traffic. "Yeah, I know where it's at. Okay." She hung up and busted a U-turn.

"Where we going?" Keishana asked.

"To a doctor's house, someone that knows my mom."

They pulled up to a two-story house in an affluent neighborhood on the south side of Miami. As soon as they pulled up, the garage door opened and Kiki pulled in. There was a pretty thick brown-skinned older lady waiting for them.

"Bring him in," she told Kiki and Keishana.

She led them into the house and into the basement, where it was set up like a major hospital. They helped her undress Taz and get him onto the hospital bed.

"Is there anything we can do?" asked Keishana

"No. He'll be out for a few hours from the sedative I gave him," she said while dressing Taz's wounds.

"And your name is?" Kiki said

"Jamie," she replied without turning around.

"You make sure you take care of my brother," Kiki said before walking out with Keishana. Kiki was about to make someone feel the pain she was feeling.

Nicholas Lock

Chapter 6

"It's hot as hell," Kiki said, wiping the sweat out of her face

She was sitting in a tree outside of a house in an upscale neighborhood in Tucson, Arizona. It took her an hour just to get over the eight foot tall fence that the neighborhood was encased in. The armed security guards made rounds every ten minutes, so she had to scale the fence and hide before they came through. It didn't help that most of the people in the neighborhood had dogs, so every time she made a noise, a dog would bark. She was dressed in an all-black catsuit like the one Halle Berry wore in *Catwoman*. Kiki regretted wearing it now because it was a hundred degrees and it was eleven o' clock at night.

The tree was right beside the house, so the jump from the tree to the balcony was only about a foot. She looked at her watch and knew she only had about thirty seconds before the security rounds would be coming. She used a knife to pop open the balcony door and crept inside. She looked around and noticed she was in a bedroom, but when she looked at the bed, it was empty. She continued through the house until she got to the master bedroom. She tiptoed until she was at the edge of the bed and stared down at the sleeping figure. Kiki wanted to just cut his throat and be done with it, but that wouldn't have been any fun. She snatched the comforter back, causing him to sit up and meet Kiki's six inch blade.

"What the fuck?" he said as Kiki held the knife to his neck.

"Don't you fucking holler. You're going to have plenty of time for that," she hissed. "Now turn over."

"Do you know who I am?"

"Yes, Juan, I do. I know you're the head of the Mexican cartel, standing in the place of your father. I'm surprised you don't know who I am," Kiki said, turning on the lamp by the bed, but maintaining knife contact

"I didn't make that call. My father did! I like Taz!" He started to plead his case upon seeing Kiki.

"Shut up and turn over!" She got mad hearing him say Taz's name.

Juan turned over. Kiki zip tied his hands behind his back and sat him up on the edge of the bed.

"Now what you're going to do is give me your dad's location and a money incentive not to kill you."

"I can't give you my father's location, but I got a million in cash in the trunk of my Phantom."

"You can't or you won't?" Kiki asked, sitting in his lap.

"What do you mean?" He was caught off-guard by her display of affection

"I'm done playing." Kiki stood up and plunged the knife into his thigh.

"Aaahh, you stupid bitch!" he screamed, rolling around the bed

Kiki hopped on top of him, pinning him to the bed.

"Why the name calling, Juan?" she asked, cutting his shirt off, then his pants, leaving him in only his boxers. "Now we can do this the easy way or the hard way." Kiki stole one of Taz's lines.

"Fuck you and Taz!" Juan spat.

"If that's how you want it."

While Juan was still in pain from the wound to his thigh, Kiki tied his feet to each bedpost, then she sat on his chest, making him lie flat.

"Now I'm going to cut the zip ties and you're going to tie your right hand to the bedpost by the headboard," Kiki said and then got up.

Kiki cut the zip ties and tossed him some torn sheets to tie his wrist up. He tied his right, then Kiki tied his left. Kiki looked into Juan's eyes and saw they had a distant look in them, as if he had resigned himself to his fate. Kiki cut his boxers off, leaving him naked.

"You still don't want to save yourself?" asked Kiki as she cupped his balls in her hand.

Juan didn't respond. He just stared at the ceiling. Kiki took the knife and slit his nut sac open.

"Aaahh!" he yelled

Kiki dug her hand in his sac until she pulled both his nuts out. She started shaking them in her hand as if they were dice.

"This is only the beginning of what I can and will do to you, so tell me what I want to know and it'll all be over," Kiki said, continuing to play with his balls.

"He has a house in the Hamptons, a penthouse in Manhattan, a mansion in Mexico, houses in Dallas and L.A., and a condo in D.C.," Juan said, barely conscious.

"Addresses?"

"My phone," he said and then passed out.

Kiki grabbed his phone and got the addresses out. As she was putting it down, it rang. When Kiki saw the name and picture that popped up, her temperature went through the roof. She went to the bed and stuck the knife through Juan's throat, killing him. Kiki then went to the garage and checked the trunk of his Phantom. Sure enough, there was a duffel bag full of money. She grabbed the bag and walked right out the front door with murder still on her mind.

***

"It's good to see you awake, Mr. Taz," Jamie said.

"Where am I?" Taz asked, seeing all the medical equipment

"My basement. Keosha and your friend brought you here two days ago. It seems you have some very powerful and resourceful enemies."

"Not as powerful as me," he said, sitting up.

He felt his chest where the choppa bullet had gone in and winced. He was still in pain, but it was bearable. The last thing he remembered was getting shot, waking up in the hospital, then getting shot again. He had to get out of there and into the battlefield. Hector had tried to get him smoked, so now there was going to be some real live gunsmoke. Hector thought he couldn't get smoked because he was at the top of the food chain, but he was about to get a first class reality check.

"Whoa, wait a minute. Where are you going?" Jamie asked as Taz tried to stand up.

"I got some things to handle." He tried standing up, but fell into Jamie.

"You need more rest," said Jamie, helping him back onto the bed.

"Yo, who the hell are you?"

"My name is Jamie and I'm a medical doctor. Kiana told me she needed a favor, then Keosha brought you over. Now get some rest."

Any other time Taz would've made a smart remark, but his whole body was sore and he didn't have the energy. He was going to check that shit when he woke up, he told himself before dozing off.

A few hours later, Taz woke up to an argument going on between Kiki and her mom.

"No! If you kill her, you're going to have a bigger problem on your hands than the Mexican cartel. Keep in mind she's carrying his child," Kiki said.

"Jamie can save the child. That's no issue. You killed Juan, so that leaves Isabella as his only child. Killing her would cripple him emotionally and then he will start making mistakes, which'll give us a shot at killing him." Ms. Kiana stated some truths.

The whole time they were going back and forth, Taz had gotten himself out of the bed and made his way up the stairs to where they were.

"Ms. Kiana, if you kill Bella, I'll kill all your kids, then your husband, and save you for last." Taz caught them off guard

"What are you doing out of bed?" Jamie asked.

"Minding my business," said Taz, struggling to make it up the last few stairs. "You killed Juan?"

"Yeah, them his nuts in that box right there." Kiki pointed to a box on the end table.

"Okay then!"

"Taz, I understand Bella is your girl, but do you think she really loves you?" Ms. Kiana questioned.

"Ms. Kiana, it's not a doubt in my mind," he said. They locked eyes.

There was a battle of wills going on. Ms. Kiana was a true alpha, but so was Taz. Neither one of them was willing to give an inch of power away, and Taz had made his mind up that he was going to have to impose his will in this war. Ms. Kiana knew Taz was the real deal. She could tell by looking into his eyes. But she'd met a hundred killers in her life and she always came out on top. She could tell Taz was different though. He had a different vibe. He respected her, but didn't fear her, and it always made her pussy wet because all the other men she ran into feared her. Being the head honcho in a crime syndicate made her feel untouchable, but Taz was shaking that up.

"First, just call me Kiana, and I guess we can look into other avenues as far as getting to Hector. But we need to do something, because he's fucking up my cash flow."

"You guess? Nah. Isabella is off the table! If I even think you got Bella in your sights, it's going to be a misunderstanding."

Kiana looked at him in disbelief. No one had ever talked to her in that manner and lived. She nodded her head as if she understood.

Taz knew that Hector always, without fail, did his business from the penthouse in Manhattan on Mondays and Tuesdays. He was about to make sure Hector received a little present this Monday.

"Now Kiki, this what I want you to do with that nigga's nuts," Taz told Kiki.

***

Three days later

"Mr. Vasquez, I have a package for you," Hector's secretary told him.

"Just set it on my desk," he said from the bathroom.

Hector came out of the bathroom and went straight to the floor to ceiling window that looked out over downtown New York. He was on top of the world. He ran the most ruthless cartel in Mexico and had the most successful import/export business in South America. And now he was in the process of moving his business to the U.S. Not to mention he was a multi-billionaire. Life couldn't get any better, plus he was about to knock off his cartel's main adversary in the States.

He walked over to his desk and picked up the package. He sat down and opened it up only for his heart to hit the floor. Hector picked up the note that was inside. It read, "Taz sends his regards. No nuts, no glory." He saw a pair of nuts in the bottom of the box. He already knew who they belonged to.

Nicholas Lock

Chapter 7

"Oh my God, baby! I've been worried sick. We've been worried sick," Bella said to Taz, clutching her stomach.

"Daddy!" His daughters rushed into the room

"Hey babies!" He picked them up, even though it hurt.

"I got all A's on my report card!" D'Azia bragged.

"That's good, baby. And what you got Neveah?"

"A's, B's, and a C," she moped.

"That's okay, but you're going to bring that C up, right?" Taz questioned, and she nodded her head. "Go get dressed while I talk to Bella."

He walked into their bedroom and sat on the bed. Bella tried to walk between his legs, but he pushed her away. Before he allowed her to get on some lovey dovey shit, he had to see where her mind was. There was a war going on and she was smack dab in the middle of it, whether she knew it or not. On the chessboard, Bella would be the queen because she had the power to change the whole game. If she were to swing Taz's way, the war would be over.

"You see what the fuck your people did to me!" Taz raised his shirt to show her the scar from the choppa bullet.

"I know, and I haven't talked to my father since I heard," she confessed running her hand over the scar.

"So you ready to help me end this?" Taz inquired, finally allowing her to walk between his legs

"Baby, stop trying to make me choose. Isn't it bad enough you killed my brother, my only brother? But I expected that after I heard you had gotten shot, which drove me crazy, by the way, especially when you didn't call me," said Bella as tears began to fall from her eyes. "If I asked you to choose between me and Kiki, would you?" She put her nose to his so they were eye to eye.

That is a good question, Taz thought to himself. In the back of his mind, he knew if he really had to choose, he would choose Kiki. The only reason he'd pause to even consider Bella was because of his son in her stomach, but he couldn't tell her that.

"I wouldn't," he lied.

"Just like I won't," she countered

"Okay, we're dressed, Daddy, now what?" Neveah burst into the room.

"Okay, y'all wait in the living room. We about to go to Disneyworld."

"Yaaayy!" They ran off squealing

"Now what's up with my son?"

"He's getting on my nerves kicking me. He'll be here in about three weeks. Am I invited on your Disneyworld trip?"

"Get dressed," Taz said, walking out of the room.

***

"Oh, so while I'm in the trenches, you going on trips to Disneyworld and shit." Kiki sat atop his Ferrari.

"Kiki, I had to spend some quality time with my daughters. Do you mind?" he asked, slapping her on the ass.

"TK said they about out of work and the plug they used to have not trying to fuck with them. My mom think it got something to do with Hector."

Since Juan had gotten killed, Hector had turned the heat all the way up. He'd had fifteen of OTF"s spots hit and had killed at least twelve of their workers. He was pulling one of Taz's moves and hitting the trap spots, which was messing up the money intake. The tides had turned in the Mexican Cartel's favor. One more major blow would knock OTF to its

50

knees. And since Hector's cartel controlled a majority of the drugs coming into the U.S., their options were slim.

"We're going to figure something out. We always do. Right now we need to find out how we're going to help Hector reunite with his son Juan," Taz said, turning into downtown Miami.

"I got all Hector's major addresses right here. That's how I know his office address. It's something else I need to holler at you about, but I have to fact check it first. What's good with your Mexican?"

"She good. I got her. You just let me handle her." He looked over at her to make sure she understood

BEEP! BEEP! BEEP! Taz turned to see Quanesha in the lane beside him blowing her horn. He pulled over and got out. Quanesha ran and jumped her Amazon ass into his arms.

"Oh God, bae! I was losing my mind!"

"Get down, girl, I'm still healing up."

She got down, but still kept her arms around his neck. Then she noticed Kiki in the passenger seat and moved her hands.

"You good, girl, that's my brother," Kiki eased her mind.

"Are you okay?" Nesha asked Taz.

"I'm good, you?"

"Now that I know my boo good, I'm good. And since you good, that means I'm going to get me some in the near future, right?" She ran her hands over his chest.

"We going to see. Now bye, girl, I'll call you later."

She kissed him on the lips then strutted away.

"She catching feelings like I told you she would," Kiki told him when he got back in the car.

"What makes you think that?"

"It's clear as day. Call it a woman's intuition."

"So what, Kiki? Mind your business. Hello?" he answered his phone.

"I'll be there in ten minutes."

"Who was that?" Kiki wanted to know.

"Johnny, and he said he need to talk to me right now. It's important."

"You think it's a set-up?" she asked, checking the clips to her pistols.

"I doubt it, but we about to see."

They pulled into Primo's Pizza and everything looked normal, but Taz still reached in the back and put on a bulletproof vest under his Ralph Lauren button-up. As soon as they walked in, Johnny ushered them into his office.

"Listen, Taz, I heard about what happened to you and who you're up against. And in my opinion, you're in need of some assistance - some heavy assistance," Johnny stated.

"And what kind of assistance can you offer?" asked Kiki.

"I can show you better than I can tell you," Johnny said.

The office door opened and a short, older Italian dude walked in. "Taz, this is my uncle Vincent, but everyone calls him Vinnie Two Times and he's a capo in the Italian Mafia."

Chapter 8

"What kind of assistance could you possibly give me?" Taz asked, confused.

"You have issues with the Mexican Cartel and so does the Mafia. You need drugs, and I have it. The enemy of my enemy is a friend to me," Vinnie told Taz.

"What's your issue with Hector?" Kiki inquired.

"He's been poking his nose where it doesn't belong. Hector's trying to wiggle his way into the gambling sector and he's not welcome. We've warned him off, but he told us to go fuck ourselves."

"So basically you want us to do your dirty work for you?" Taz spoke his mind.

"I wouldn't put it like that. You need us and we need you, so it works both ways. What do you have to lose?"

Taz looked at Kiki and she nodded her head at him as if to say it was on him. Taz knew they needed this, especially TK and them, but what would the ultimate cost be? Getting in the bed with Hector and the Mexican Cartel had started off good, but now that same relationship was turning his world upside down. If they started rocking with the Mafia, what was going to happen if they fell out?

"Let's just say we do decide to team up. What's going to happen if I decide to cut ties once this is over?"

"Absolutely nothing. We'll have Hector and his cartel out of our hair and you'll be free to do as you please," Vinnie eased Taz's mind.

"How much cocaine can you provide and what's the quality?" Kiki asked.

"We can provide however much you need and the quality is top notch. Hector isn't the only one with high grade coke," he bragged.

"I was under the impression the mob didn't deal in drugs," Taz said.

Vinnie laughed before saying, "You read too many books. Believe half of what you see and none of what you hear."

Taz and Kiki left the meeting with a new plug and some much-needed intel on Hector and his moves. One thing Taz had learned from dealing with these kingpins and other bosses was that they weren't to be trusted. If they thought they could pull a fast one on you, they usually did. Taz was going to see to it that once they dealt with Hector, he was cutting ties with the Mafia.

***

Isabella had Taz's son on June 13, 2018. He was nine pounds, three ounces. They named him D'angelo Walker Junior. He looked just like Taz except he had Isabella's skin tone. Taz and Kiki were in the room while Bella breastfed Junior. The only reason Isabella wasn't protesting was because Taz told her if she caused a scene, he'd leave and take Junior with him, and he put it on Tyshae so Bella knew he was serious. Since Taz had gotten shot, Kiki wouldn't let Taz out of her sights.

After Bella got done feeding Junior, Taz grabbed him up so he could hold him for a while. Taz could feel the heat coming off Isabella as she looked in Kiki's direction. They were going to bump heads in the future, and this time he was going to let it play itself out.

As Taz was rocking his son, Hector appeared in the doorway and Kiki shot to her feet.

"You got a lot of balls, wetback." Kiki clutched her hammer

"Tsk, tsk, tsk. Such language in front of my grandson."

"Your grandson? He'll never know you," Taz said without looking up from Junior's face,

"I'm not worried about your idle threats," Hector said confidently, making Taz's blood boil

"Quit it! My son's in here!" Bella screamed, causing Junior to cry.

Taz gave Junior to Bella to quiet him down and Taz pulled his pistol out.

"What's to stop me from blowing your brains out?" said Taz as he slowly raised his gun.

"You mean beside the fact that you won't leave this hospital alive? You might want to go look out the window."

Taz moved to the window with his gun still pointed at Hector and looked out the window. There were about fifty of Hector's people milling around so it looked as if Hector was going to miss his date with the Grim Reaper.

"Get the fuck out of here! Now!" Taz yelled, mad that the source of his problems was right in front of him and he couldn't do shit about it.

"Did you like the gift box we sent you? You'll have another one real soon," said Kiki, cutting her grey eyes towards Bella.

Hector acted as if he wanted to say something, but he walked out instead.

Just as soon as he walked out, Isabella said, "Bitch, when I heal up, I'm going to beat you to death."

Kiki looked to Taz and he shook his head, signaling to her not to say anything.

"Bella, go ahead with that shit," Taz warned her.

Taz was getting sick and tired of her picking fights with Kiki. He could understand if she was fucking with her over some legit shit, but she was on some jealous shit. She was going to mess around and make him leave her alone, especially with the way Nesha was sexing him.

"You always taking her side." Bella started to pout.

"If you say so. Anyway, the doctor said we could take Junior home. Are you ready?"

"Yeah, let me grab my stuff."

They gathered her things up and took off. It was going to feel funny having a baby in the house after all this time. It had been a long time since Taz had to change a diaper, but he was up for it. Taz finally had the son he wanted.

"She's not sitting in the back with my baby," Bella said, as they walked out the front of the hospital

"Well, you can get your ass in the back then, Bella, with your petty-acting ass," said Taz, carrying Junior.

When they were about fifty feet from Taz's CT6, he hit the button on his keychain to start the car and the car blew up, knocking them backwards, but Taz was sure to shield his son. When the smoke cleared, all that was left of his car was a mangled piece of steel. Taz looked to Bella to make sure she understood the magnitude of what had just happened. If they would've been in the car, they all would've died, including his son. It was time to up the ante.

Chapter 9

Enough was enough! Taz and Kiki were about to hit Hector's pocket in a major way. Pillow talking with Bella had revealed one of Hector's drug warehouses. Whether she realized it or not, she'd given Taz some major information. Yesterday Vinnie had delivered on his end of the deal and delivered them some grade-A cocaine plus some loud, which shut TK, Reggie, and PJ up. Now it was time for Taz to begin to deliver on his end. They were in Houston's port, looking for the right warehouse. There were so many.

"This shit is going to take forever," Taz said looking at all the warehouses. "We might have to go through each one."

"Or we could just go to the one that all those esse's just left from." Kiki pointed.

"Fuck you,"

"Nah, I'm straight," she smirked.

"We're going to come back later on tonight and fuck his world up."

They pulled out and went back to their hotel. When they got to their room, Taz got in the bed to try and get some rest, but Kiki wasn't having it. She was in one of her playful moods. She started jumping on his bed, preventing him from going to sleep.

"You know you too big for this," Taz said from under the covers.

"You ain't spent no time with me in the last few months, so now you don't have a choice." She continued to jump around on his bed.

She was right. He hadn't been spending enough time with her. He'd had so much going on. They usually made time to see each other on a daily basis. Bella had started accusing them of the same thing his ex-girlfriend Candace used to, saying he and Kiki were fucking, but they just didn't understand the bond he and Kiki had.

"Stop jumping on my damn bed!" He sat up

"Well, get up."

"Go roll up," he said.

They'd gotten some weed from a nigga at a gas station and he said it was called rocket kush. He said it would take you to the moon, and Taz was trying to find out. While Kiki rolled up, Taz cut the Jacuzzi on. If he couldn't get any sleep, at least he could relax. He stripped down to his boxers and got in.

"Oh, that ain't fair, I ain't got no bikini."

"Put on a pair of my boxers. Ain't like you ain't never put them on before."

"I'm not putting them stanking-ass shits on."

"Good. I don't want you messing up my relaxation no way. Pass the bud."

Taz took two pulls of the weed just as Kiki climbed in the Jacuzzi naked, causing him to start coughing.

"You never cease to amaze me," said Taz, regaining his composure.

"You've seen me naked a zillion times. What's one more?"

"You was a nigga in another lifetime. You act too much like one not to have been," he told her while passing her the blunt.

"So this is the plan. We're going to hit this warehouse tonight, then the warehouse in Miami, then the ones in New York and Mexico."

"Kiki, do you ever give your mind a break? You can't be on go mode 24/7. Take a day off. You need a vacation."

"A vacation? Never heard of it. What's that? I'm thugging with no brakes! I'll take a vacation after I kill Hector," Kiki said matter-of-factly,

"No, you're going to take one when I tell you to. I been gone that long that you motherfuckers forgot who the boss is." Taz felt himself getting mad.

He climbed out of the Jacuzzi and grabbed a towel to dry off. Taz was going to have to reassert himself because that was the second time he had been questioned, and it was also going to be the last time. Him playing the background had obviously given niggas the impression that shit was sweet. He was going to show them just how sweet it was, starting with Kiki.

"You think I'm soft or something? You think I ain't got it no more?"

He blanked. "Why you yelling at me?"

"That's all you motherfuckers seem to understand is me yelling and violence. Let me see that towel." Kiki tried to grab for the towel. "Go ahead now, I'm serious."

Taz moved the towel out of her reach. "Bitch, you got me fucked up!" Taz snapped.

Taz grabbed her and slammed her on the bed. She tried to get up, but Taz punched her in the ribs, letting her know he was serious. Kiki started going crazy trying to scratch and punch him.

"I'm not to be played with," he warned. "What I say goes. Now go put some fucking clothes on," Taz said, letting her up.

POP! POP! POP! Kiki hit him with a three piece that busted his lip. Taz grabbed her by the neck and slung her back on the bed.

"I know what your stupid-ass problem is. I don't know why it took me so long, but I got your ass," he said, stepping out of his boxers.

Kiki tried to get up off the bed, but Taz pushed her back down and got between her legs.

"Get the fuck off me," Kiki said through clenched teeth.

Taz put his hand between her legs and flicked his thumb across her clit, making her jump. Then he ran his fingers down her clit only for his fingers to come away dripping wet. Taz slipped a finger inside her.

"Stop, Taz." Kiki grabbed his wrist, but was humping his finger.

Taz used his fingers to guide himself to Kiki's love box. He tried to enter her, but she was too tight. He sucked one of her double D's into his mouth and she cried out.

"Oh Taz, this is so wrong," she moaned while pushing his head lower.

When he got face to face with her pussy, she put her feet on his shoulders and her hands in his dreads. Taz blew on her pussy and her lips opened all the way up, showing him her pink insides. He tongue kissed her clit while sliding two fingers in and out of her.

"Oh my God!" she yelled. "Make me cum, Taz!"

Taz drew his name in cursive on her clit with his tongue, sending her into a frenzy. Kiki started throwing her head from side to side as Taz ate her pussy with wild abandon

"It's coming," Kiki moaned as she coated Taz's face.

Taz got back in between her legs, lining himself up with her pussy.

"Let me taste my pussy." Kiki grabbed him and licked his face before sticking her tongue in his mouth.

While they kissed, Taz got the head in, but couldn't get in any further.

"Why your pussy so tight?"

Kiki dug her nails into his back as he worked his way in deeper. Taz grabbed one of Kiki's legs and lifted it up, opening her up. Once he got all the way in, Taz went to work. Taz started plunging in and out of Kiki, causing her to put her hand on the bottom of his stomach, trying to control his strokes.

"Nah, move your hand. Grab them big-ass titties while I tame this cat."

Kiki did what he said and grabbed her breast, pulling one to her mouth and licking her nipple.

"Freaky bitch, take all this dick!"

Taz lifted both her legs and long stroked her. He was going all the way in until his balls stopped up against her ass.

"Let me ride it."

Taz got up and laid on his back so she could climb on top. Kiki went to rocking her hips in a circular motion. Taz hadn't had pussy that clenched his dick like this in a long time. It felt like her pussy was made for his dick. Kiki leaned up and started popping her ass up and down, bringing Taz to the verge of busting.

"Hold up, bend over. You not going to get off without me getting this ass from the back."

Kiki got up and bent over. Taz grabbed his dick, getting ready to put it in, when he noticed what looked like blood on his dick.

"I know you not on your period!"

"Hell no, nigga!"

"What the fuck you bleeding for then?"

"You popped my cherry, nigga, duh! Why you think this pussy so tight?" She said as if it was no big deal, catching Taz off-guard.

Hearing that brought Taz to his senses. He was fucking Kiki, something they had both vowed not to do. They were in the wrong, plus he'd just taken her virginity, something he wasn't really sure she still had. This was going to change their relationship in more ways than one.

"Nigga, fuck your pussy and quit playing." Kiki tried to get Taz to go back in her, but he wasn't having it.

Taz got up, put his clothes on, and walked out to get his mind right because what they'd done was irreversible and Taz knew there was going to be some kind of backlash to their act.

Chapter 10

"Get your ass up!" Taz kicked the bed, waking Kiki up

Taz had spent the night in another room because he didn't want to go back to the room with Kiki. He was up all night trying to figure out what had gone wrong between the two of them, but couldn't come up with an answer. All that had happened last night was going to have to be put behind them because it was business time now. They'd already fucked up by not hitting the warehouse last night. So now they had to hit it in the daytime, which added another element of risk. Taz had stolen an NRG Energy van to try and help them gain access to the warehouse instead of storming in guns blazing.

"Put this on and hurry up," Taz told Kiki, handing her an NRG Energy uniform.

She didn't protest. She got up and put the uniform on without a word.

There was no need for them to make a plan. They'd pulled so many moves together that they knew what the other was going to do. Taz and Kiki pulled up to the warehouse just as a van was pulling out.

"What do you want?" a Mexican asked when they pulled up to the entrance.

"There's been a gas leak in the area and we have to check all the warehouses in the area," Taz told him

He looked in the front of the van from Taz to Kiki as if inspecting them. After a few seconds, he said, "Unlock the back"

Taz unlocked the back of the van. The Mexican peeked in. Satisfied, he spoke into his walkie-talkie and spoke some Spanish, telling whoever was inside to cover everything up. Taz's Spanish was now superb. He could understand and speak it fluently now. When the esse got the okay, he opened the warehouse doors, letting the fox into the henhouse. Driving in, Taz only counted ten esse's standing around in various spots.

"Follow my lead," he told Kiki before they got out of the van.

Taz and Kiki walked to the back of the van and grabbed the meters used for detecting gas vapors. Taz went to one end of the warehouse and Kiki to the other, acting as if they were scanning for a gas leak. Taz had expected some of the esse's to follow them around, but they stayed stationary. They were going to have to improvise. Reading Taz's mind, Kiki started making a commotion on the other side, causing all the esse's to run to where she was. While Kiki had their attention, Taz came up behind them and cocked the twin Desert Eagles he had concealed in his uniform.

"First one moves is the first one who gets shot," he said as Kiki relieved them of their weapons "On your knees!"

Taz and Kiki tied all their hands behind their backs and their legs together. Taz walked over to one of the tables and snatched the tarp off.

"Jackpot!" Taz yelled, seeing all the bricks laid out on the table.

"Holy shit!" Kiki said, taking the tarp off another table and seeing pounds and pounds of weed.

Taz pulled the tarps off all the tables and it was more of the same thing: bricks of coke and pounds of weed. But the last table was all money, making this the biggest lick he or Kiki had ever hit in their life. Furthermore, this was the most money he'd ever seen or had, and he could tell that just by looking at it. While Taz was gawking at the money, Kiki had started loading the van up.

"Are you going to help?" she asked.

Taz nodded his head and started loading the money into the back. It took them almost an hour to get everything inside the van. Taz was nervous as hell pulling out because they had enough drugs to get them a few life sentences. This was the kind of lick that head niggas dreamed about. This was one of those licks you retired off of. It was also one of those that if it came out that it was you, you'd best move your family. This was going to be a major blow to Hector, and this was just the tip of the iceberg.

***

"Check it out! This is how this shit is going down from now on. I'm calling all the shots! By the time all this is over with, if you haven't found a legit way to get money, then that's on you! But don't call my phone when you get in some bull-shit. That goes for you too. Kiki." Taz told them.

Taz had gotten everybody to meet him at one of Kiki's houses in Atlanta. He was letting them know he was back in charge.

"I don't know why you trying to single me out." Kiki scrunched her face up.

He ignored her and said, "Do anybody got an issue with what I said?"

Everybody shook their heads, letting him know everything was good.

"Damn, what's going on here?" Meosha, Kiki's identical twin, barged into the house.

And she was looking like a million bucks! She had on some yellow boy shorts with the words "like that" across the ass, a yellow halter top that was cut so the bottom of her titties were visible, and some white and yellow 7's. The yellow stood out against her dark skin, making her look even better. Her having a key to Kiki's house surprised him because just a few months ago, they were at each other's necks.

"What's up, twin?" Kiki asked.

"Cooling, about to raid your closet for something to wear tonight. You know Future performing tonight at Club Platinum."

"Where my 'what's up' at?" PJ asked Meosha.

"Hey PJ, TK, and Reggie, where you been stranger?" She walked up to Taz with her arms out for a hug

Kiki stepped in front of Taz before Meosha could hug him.

"Damn, sis! I just want a hug." Meosha smiled "Oh, and Taz, my mama want to talk to you," she said before disappearing into Kiki's bedroom.

Taz called Kiana to see what she wanted to talk to him about.

"I need to talk to you in person. I'm going to be at Club Platinum tonight," she said and then hung up

Taz looked at the phone and frowned. She was going to be another one that he was going to have to get an understanding with. It was clear that she thought he was one of her flunkies. He was about to clear that up ASAP.

"Meosha, where your mama at?"

"At the office," she yelled from the bedroom.

Taz took off out the door without saying anything to anybody. He made it to Kiana's office in less than ten minutes. He was in such a hurry he took the steps instead of waiting on the elevator. With every story he climbed, he got madder and madder. When he came out of the stairwell, he saw the same secretary that tried to deny him the last time. When she saw Taz, her eyes got big, but she didn't say anything, nor did she try to stop him from walking into the back.

Taz barged into Kiana's office and slammed and locked the door. Kiana was on the phone and Taz took the phone out of her hands and slammed it down.

"What the fuck do you think you're doing?" she yelled, jumping up.

"You got me fucked up! I'm not one of your flunkies that you can handle any kind of way," he blanked.

"I do what the fuck I want to, to who I want to, when I want to," Kiana said, coming around her desk with a chrome .45

"Don't no fear pump in my blood!" Taz walked up on her until she put the gun to his forehead "You the one with the pussy! I got the dick and balls!" he said, grabbing his dick.

"Don't think I won't kill you," Kiana said calmly, looking Taz in the eyes.

"You ain't did it yet! When I pull my gun, I use it!" Taz tried her.

When he saw she wasn't going to shoot, he turned around to walk out and she punched him in the back of the head. Taz didn't believe in putting his hands on women, but between Kiki and her mama were testing that belief. Then a thought occurred to him. Taz was a firm believer that most women that acted like Kiana dealt with inferior men and just needed a real nigga to blow their back out. In his past experiences, after you fucked them real good, they submitted. Taz spun around, grabbed the gun with one hand, and choked her with the other. She dropped the gun and Taz put both hands around her neck, lifting her off her feet.

"I told your ass I'm not one of your flunkies," he growled.

Kiana wrapped her legs around him, trying to ease the pressure around her neck. Taz set her down and took one of his hands off her neck.

"I'm going to kill you." She gasped for air.

Taz put his hands under her business skirt and ripped her panties off.

"Are you out of your mind?" Kiana screamed, trying to move.

Taz began to squeeze her neck again. He bit on her lip to keep her from screaming again and guided his dick inside her love box.

"Mmmm," she moaned.

Taz pulled her up and turned her around. He wasn't here to make love. He was about to fuck her into submission. Taz kicked her feet apart and bent her over.

"Grab your ankles," he demanded.

Kiana reached down, grabbed her ankles, looked back at him, and said, "Now what, nigga?"

Taz grabbed her hips and pushed in until his hips were up against her ass. Her pussy was so wet, he was going to need all his willpower to keep from going over the deep end.

"Too much for you, little boy."

Taz pulled back and started slamming into her for all he was worth.

"Yeah! Yeah! Yeah!" she yelled.

Taz grabbed a handful of her hair and began hitting her with long, hard strokes.

"Yeah, bitch, take this dick! Like I said, I got the dick and you got the pussy," he said, speeding up.

As Taz sped his strokes up. She started trying to run. Kiana rose up on her toes as if that was going to slow Taz down.

"Wait a minute," she said, trying to walk forward.

Taz let her walk forward until she was up against the window in her office that overlooked the parking lot. Taz let her stand up straight and went back to pounding away at her insides. Kiana braced herself on the window with her hands while Taz fucked her into the strongest orgasm she'd had in her life. Her juices ran down Taz's dick all over his Balmain shorts. Kiana went limp and Taz caught her by the waist and kept stroking.

"Get on your knees," he told her, getting ready to nut.

Kiana got on her knees and Taz put his dick down her throat until she gagged and her eyes watered. Taz showed her no mercy. He fucked her mouth the same way he fucked her pussy.

"I'm about to nut, bitch, and you better swallow it," Taz said, grabbing the back of her head.

Taz pumped a few more times and then released what felt like a gallon of his sperm down her throat. Kiana didn't miss a beat. She swallowed every drop then made it a point to lick her lips.

"Recognize a boss when you see one," Taz said, zipping his pants up and walking out, leaving Kiana on her knees with a sore pussy and a sticky mouth.

Nicholas Lock

Chapter 11

Taz left Atlanta after his episode with Kiana. He wanted to get back to his son and his babies. Just as soon as he got to Miami, Quanesha called his phone

"What's up, baby girl?"

"Nothing, just laying here thinking about you. I need to talk to you too," she said, giving Taz some pause.

Every time he heard "I need to talk", it was always some bad shit. He could only imagine what it had to do with.

"I'll be there in a minute" he said and hung up.

Taz didn't have time for any more bullshit. He was at his limit. He pulled up to her apartment on campus and saw a bunch of dread heads standing around the parking lot. He put one in the head of his hammer and got out.

Nesha opened the door before Taz could even knock. As usual, she was looking good.

"Hey boo." She kissed him and let him in.

"What's up, Nesha?" He hugged her from behind, sucking on her neck.

"I needed to see you, baby." She turned around so she was facing him. "I been lonely. It's like you neglecting me."

"Don't start catching feelings, Nesha."

"What you mean?" She narrowed her eyes.

"Just what I said. Let's not complicate what we got going on."

"Whatever." She stormed off to her bedroom.

Taz took a deep breath. He really wasn't in the mood to deal with females and their emotions. He walked into the bedroom and Nesha was lying across the bed flipping through the channels. She rolled her eyes when she saw him.

"You supposed to be mad now?" he asked, grinning.

Nesha kept flipping through the channels, ignoring him, so he laid down beside her. She tried to scoot away from him, but he grabbed her and pulled her back to him.

"Get off me, Taz."

"That's how you're going to do me?"

"It's how you're doing me."

"Cut that shit out!" Taz pulled her on top of him. "I thought we had an understanding that we was just cooling it. You knew I had a lady and you was cool with it, so why all this shit now?"

"It ain't my fault I caught feelings. It's yours! Maybe if you came over, fucked me, and left, but you be cuddling with me. You be treating me like I'm your girl. Staying the night with me, taking me shopping… Nigga, you bought me the new Porsche truck!"

Taz thought about everything she was saying and she was making a valid point. Maybe he was leading her on. Her beauty had put him under a spell. Maybe it was time to start falling back from her because he wasn't about to let her fuck up his happy home. He was going to have to fuck her one more time though.

"What do you want me to do?" he asked.

"I don't know." She laid down on his chest.

"I know what I want you to do," Taz said. He started pushing her head down until it was in his lap.

Nesha reached in his pants and went to work. That was another thing that had him under her thumb. Whenever Taz wanted his dick sucked, she did it with no questions asked, and when he wanted some pussy, she'd give it to him whether she was on her period or not.

Taz laid back and let her suck his dick in a way only she and Victoria could. They gave that porno head. Taz released in Nesha's mouth and rolled over to take a power nap before he headed home.

***

"You going to spoil him. You're not supposed to hold them while they sleep." Kiki tried to coach Taz on a subject she knew nothing about.

"When did you become an expert at childcare?" asked Taz, putting Junior down in his bassinet.

It was just Taz, Kiki, and Junior at the house. He'd given Bella a break. She'd taken his daughters Neveah and D'Azia out with her to do some shopping and get their nails done. They were basically going to get pampered. This was the first time he and Kiki had been alone since their issue in Houston. He'd been trying to avoid her because he knew how she was. It was only a matter of time before she brought it up, and Taz really wasn't trying to discuss it. And sure enough, Kiki started up.

"So you not going to fuck me no more?"

"Kiki... We weren't supposed to do that in the first place. You know we was out of order."

"How? Taz, you been my nigga whether you knew it or not! Yeah, we brother and sister for play-play, but in all actuality, we're not related. So us fucking shouldn't be an issue! I love you just as much as I know you love me! I know bean eating-ass Isabella is your girl and she has your heart to a certain extent, as do I. So since I can't get it wholly, I'm going to get this dick when I need it," she said in her usual straight forward manner.

This was not going to turn out well. Many men would love to be in this position, but Taz knew it would most likely end in disaster because there were feelings involved already. Taz and Kiki already loved each other, but that was before they fucked. If they started having sex on a regular basis, those feelings would most likely skyrocket, which would further complicate the situation.

"Look at our nails, Daddy!" Taz's daughters rushed into the house, waving their hands in his face.

"They're pretty," he said. "Y'all better hush up before y'all wake your little brother up."

"What are you doing that close to my baby?" Bella walked in picking at Kiki.

"You're not pregnant no more, little girl," Kiki reminded her.

"What are saying?" Bella dropped her bags.

Kiki turned her head to the side, looking at her as if she was crazy.

"I'm saying whatever you think I'm saying!" Kiki shot back.

"Get fucked up!"

"Space and opportunity." Kiki held her arms out.

"Neveah, y'all go play in y'all room. Bella, y'all go outside! Now!" Taz spoke up.

Taz pulled the bassinet to the back door and they all walked outside into the backyard. Kiki took her Prada stilettos off and pulled her hair into a ponytail.

"Hold up, hold up." Taz grabbed his phone and Facetimed PJ, TK, and Reggie so they could watch the fight "A'ight, go ahead."

Kiki and Bella squared up and started circling each other. You could see Kiki had reach and weight over Bella. Kiki hit Bella with a jab that jerked her head back.

"All day, bitch!" Kiki hit her with another jab, busting her lip.

Bella got tired of her jab and rushed in. Kiki caught her with a two piece, but Bella kept coming and hit Kiki with a four piece combo that stumbled her. Bella tried to take advantage of Kiki stumbling, but Kiki regained her feet beforehand. She sidestepped Bella's advance and dropped her with an uppercut. Belle's face was red as hell.

She peeked over at Taz and yelled "Aaahh!" She rushed Kiki again, but this time she didn't stop swinging. She caught Kiki with a left hook that put her on the ground, shocking her.

"Yeah, all day, bitch!" Bella yelled.

"Ohhh shit!" TK, PJ, and Reggie screamed.

Taz just watched. He knew Bella could hold her own, but he'd taught Kiki how to fight. And he knew her hearing TK and them screaming would send her into a rage. Now they were going to see just what Bella knew because Kiki was about to cut up.

Kiki started jabbing her to death. She'd hit Bella with a jab and make it so she couldn't rush her.

"You scared, bitch?" Bella hollered, frustrated that she couldn't hit her.

"Okay, bitch, come on." Kiki planted her feet.

Bella rushed up to Kiki and they started going blow for blow. They were going toe to toe, but you could tell Kiki was bullshitting while Bella was giving it her all. Kiki was raised in the streets while Bella was only twenty-two while Kiki was twenty-seven. Kiki must've started getting tired because she ducked one of Bella's swings and came up with an uppercut that probably would've rattled Taz and dropped Isabella. She got on top of her and started getting nasty.

"Didn't I——" Pow! "Tell you——" Pow! "That you——" Pow! "Couldn't fuck——" Pow! "With me——" Pow! Kiki would hit Bella after every two words.

"It's over, Kiki." Taz made her get up. "Y'all seen that heavyweight bout?" he asked his boys. But when he looked at the screen, he saw the looks on their faces. "What's up?"

"They just killed Kiki's pops," Reggie said. "I got word just now."

Taz just hung up. Kiki and her dad weren't all that cool, but he knew how she felt about family.

"Come here, Kiki," Taz said.

"I know you not about to baby that bitch!" Bella screamed.

He ignored her and said, "Kiki, they killed your dad."

Kiki shot out of the house, obviously on her way to Atlanta. When Kiki finally did catch up to Hector, he was going to curse the day he was born.

Chapter 12

While Kiki was in Atlanta, Taz had to get back to his businesses. When he walked into Majestic Realtors, Mary and Keishana were in their offices, but upon seeing him, they rushed out to greet him.

"I'm so mad at you, nigga." Keishana hugged him. "You ain't called me to let me know you was good or nothing."

"You on some bullshit," Mary added.

"I'm here now, so what's been going on?" he asked, unlocking his office.

"Guess what deal I closed?" Keishana asked, sitting down on the sofa he had in his office.

"Which one?"

"The condo overlooking South Beach," she bragged.

"And I closed on the house in Naples," Mary boasted.

Taz checked the paperwork and just as he thought, those were million dollar deals. Majestic Realtors was quickly becoming the cream of the crop in Florida. No other real estate company was closing half the amount of high-end deals that they were.

"Y'all the MVP's of real estate."

"Oh my gosh, I meant to tell you. You know Candace died." Mary dropped a bomb.

Damn, Taz thought. The news didn't crush him like he thought it would. It still hurt him a little bit to hear it, but she had made her bed by fucking with SK when Taz went to prison. They'd become cordial, but it would've never been the same.

"The disease killed her, right?" Taz inquired.

They nodded their heads. SK had given her AIDS and it had finally taken her down. Taz looked over at Keishana and saw a tear slip down her cheek. The same fuck nigga that had given Candace AIDS was also the one that gave it to Keishana. If Taz could bring him back, he would, just to kill him again.

"Y'all are nothing alike, so wipe your face," said Taz "You take way better care of yourself than she did. Look at you! Everywhere you go, you are one of the baddest bitches in the room. And you done had it this long."

"He right, girl, cheer up," Mary cosigned.

"Fuck all this sad shit! We're going to celebrate tonight, let's hit King of Diamonds," Taz told them.

"Hell yeah! And I heard it's going to be lit tonight too," Mary said, walking out.

Keishana kept sitting on the sofa with the long face.

"Bring your ass here!"

She got up and walked around his desk to where he was at.

"You just going to stand there?" he asked, and she plopped her juicy fat ass in his lap. "Now what's wrong with you?" Taz asked, rubbing on her thick chocolate thighs.

"Nothing, Taz, I just hate that I let that nigga do me like this. And you nasty too, nigga." She looked back at him.

"What?"

"Why your dick hard?"

Taz started laughing. "Your sexy ass," said Taz, sticking his hand between her legs.

"Stooop, Taz," she moaned, grabbing his wrist.

"Nah, you need this, ride it out." Taz circled her clit through her panties, causing her to involuntarily rock her hips back and forth.

Taz added pressure to her clit with his thumb and stuck his middle finger in and out of her pussy, bringing her to an orgasm. She bit down on her lip to keep from crying out.

"I hate you, nigga. How you know I needed that?" Keishana asked, coming down from her euphoria.

"Because you don't be fucking because you don't be wanting to risk infecting nobody else. Plus I know it's a different feeling with me playing in your pussy than you doing it yourself and it's kinkier."

"Thank you," she said, kissing him on the cheek and walking out.

A lot of people would've thought Taz was crazy for what he'd just done, but Taz knew you could only get the virus through unprotected sex or an open wound. Taz went to wash his hands, then he was off to the mall to get something to wear to the strip club tonight.

***

"Where you going all dressed up?" Bella wanted to know.

"To King of Diamonds with Mary and Keishana. Be up when I get back too, because I'm trying to put another baby in you tonight."

Taz had bought a pair of black True Religion shorts with the word "True" on them in white. Then he got a black True Religion shirt with white sleeves. He already had the black and white Oreo Five's at the house.

"Bae, where my bracelet at?"

"The last time I seen it, Neveah had it."

"Neveah, bring my bracelet, little girl."

Neveah came running into the room with his bracelet. He'd had a custom bracelet made. It was seven rows of black and white VVS diamonds. The chain and bracelet together had cost him three hundred and fifty bands! Usually Taz wouldn't have spent that much, but that warehouse lick had put him and Kiki so far ahead of the game it was unreal. They had gotten two hundred pounds of loud, a hundred bricks of coke, and two and a half million dollars in cash. Kiki and Taz had split the bread. He was letting Kiki wholesale the work and they were going to split the profits. TK, PJ, and Reggie were going to be good on work for a long time.

"Give me a kiss before I go," he told Bella and she crawled across the bed to give him a kiss "Remember what I said, Bella, and y'all be good until I get back." He kissed Neveah and D'Azia.

Taz was going to drive his Ferrari, but he opted instead for the G-wagon Bella had just gotten. Her pussy-ass daddy gave it to her for her and the baby. He called to see if Mary and Keishana were going to ride with him or not. Mary was showing a client a house so she was going to be a little late, but Keishana was ready right now. Taz pulled up to Keishana's house and she walked out looking like a quarter piece. She was wearing a hot pink Fendi mini and some hot pink six inch Jimmy Choo stilettos. Her hair was in an updo and she had put something on her chocolate skin that had it glowing.

"You trying to bag something tonight, ain't you?" Taz asked.

"Shut up." She rolled her eyes and pushed him in the side of the head.

"They pulled up to King of Diamonds and saw a long-ass line.

"I'm not about to wait in that long ass line," said Keishana.

"What you got in mind?"

"I know the bouncer."

They got out and Taz followed her up to the door. Keishana and the bouncer exchanged a few words and he let them in. Taz got thirty thousand in ones and tried to give Keishana half, but she refused. They got a table in the middle against the wall. Taz ordered two bottles of Ace of Spades and waited for Mary to get there.

"What's your plan, Taz?"

"What you mean my plan?" He was confused.

"Your life plan, what is it? Because I know you're straight money-wise so why do you still play the streets? Don't you want to be able to enjoy your life? To see your kids grow up? The little things. Me having AIDS, I know my time here is limited. It makes me appreciate every day I'm here," she confessed.

He never thought about it in that aspect. He most definitely wanted to see his babies grow up. And he hadn't really enjoyed his bread like that. He had expensive items, but he wanted to do more.

"I want to be successful in all aspects. As a businessman, a father, a friend, and a husband."

"Husband?" she smiled

"Sooner or later." He grinned, showing off his icy grill.

"About time," Keishana said when Mary walked up.

"Oh, hush."

Now it was time to party! They popped open the bottles and the strippers started popping their asses. They were throwing so much money that most of the strippers migrated to their section. Taz had two strippers dancing for him and Mary and Keishana each had one. Taz was drinking Ace of Spades straight out of the bottle.

"You not drinking, Keishana?" asked Mary.

"A little bit, but the way Taz over there drinking, I'm going to have to drive us home."

"You don't want no private dance, daddy?" a thick brown-skinned stripper asked.

"What can I get in a private dance that I can't get right here?"

"Come on so I can show you." She grabbed Taz's hand and led him to the back.

Taz sat down as she bent over and started making her ass clap one cheek at a time. He grabbed both cheeks and lifted them up, exposing a pretty pink pussy. She turned around and said, "Pull it out."

"Nah, baby girl, maybe next time."

She looked like she couldn't believe it, shrugged, and went back to grinding in his lap. She finished her dance and Taz tipped her a stack, then walked back to where Mary and Keishana were. When Taz walked up, he saw Keishana had her face balled up.

"What up?"

"These thirsty-ass niggas won't leave me the fuck alone."

"Who?" Taz looked around.

"Enjoy yourself, Taz, I'm about to call me an Uber."

"Don't play me. Let's go."

They left and Keishana and Mary said their goodbyes and then went their separate ways. Taz let Keishana drive because he was tipsy.

They were at a stoplight when two trucks pulled up alongside of them. At first Taz didn't think anything of it, but then he noticed that both trucks were occupied by Mexicans.

"Keishana, run this light right now!"

"Huh? Nigga, is you crazy?"

BOOM! BOOM! BOOM! TAT! TAT! TAT!

The Mexicans started unloading shots at the G-wagon, then she took off. They took off behind her, still shooting. It seemed like every shot was hitting the wagon, but then Taz noticed not one of them had come through.

"I'll be damned," he said more to himself than Keishana.

"What?" Keishana yelled, swerving around cars, trying to get away.

"Calm down, boo, we good. The damn truck bulletproof," he said, still kind of shocked.

She slowed down a little bit and the esse's caught up and started shooting again. Then they, too, noticed that their rounds weren't penetrating. Amid their confusion, Taz rolled his window down enough to shoot the driver, sending one of the trucks careening off the road. They were able to get away from the other truck without incident, but the thing that was nagging Taz was how the fuck they knew where he was.

Nicholas Lock

Chapter 13

"What's good, sexy?"

"Just laying here in the bed."

"You going to let me come lay with you? And are you in one of your freaky moods? Because I'm going to bring Kiki with me."

"Come on," she said and then hung up.

"What, you nervous of something?" Taz questioned Kiki as they rode to Mary's house and she rolled her eyes

They rode in silence the rest of the way to Mary's house.

"Don't get in your feelings, nigga," Kiki said, getting out of the car.

Taz ignored her and rang the doorbell. Mary answered the door in a silk robe and let them in. Taz slapped her on the ass as they walked to her bedroom. Mary sat down on her bed and took off her robe, revealing a purple lingerie set. Mary was about to peel off her thong until she saw she was the only one taking her clothes off, then the looks on Taz's and Kiki's faces made her uneasy.

"Why y'all just standing there?" Mary asked nervously.

"Where your phone, Mary?" Kiki inquired.

She pointed to the nightstand and Kiki grabbed it.

"Mary, I been hearing some very unsatisfactory things and I really don't want to believe them, but the person they're coming from is someone I trust with my life," Taz stated.

"You know who killed Juan, Mary? Me. And while I was there, his phone rang, and guess whose name and picture showed up? Yours," Kiki said, thumbing through Mary's phone.

"Please let me explain!" she yelled as Taz and Kiki pulled their guns out.

Last night after Taz questioned Bella about the bulletproof G-wagon, she told him her dad didn't want her getting caught in Taz's drama so he'd gotten it bulletproofed. Then he laid in the bed all night wondering how the hell Hector's goons kept finding him. That's when Kiki called and broke the news to him about Mary. She said she waited so long because she'd wanted to be sure Mary wasn't living right.

"They took my son! They took Keishawn!" She broke down crying. "They told me if I didn't help them, they'd kill my son and send him to me in pieces."

"Why the fuck didn't you just come to me?" Taz blanked "You know my pedigree, you know I would've done everything in my power to get your son back."

"And do you really think that after they killed Taz they were going to just give you your son back?" Kiki poked her in the head with the gun.

""You know what, Mary? You about to fix this," said Taz as an idea popped into his head. "You going to call them and tell them I'm going to be working late at the office tonight."

"You sure about this?" wondered Kiki.

"I got a plan."

As Mary called to set it up, Taz told Kiki what his plan was and how they were going to execute it.

***

"They're on their way in now," Kiki said, from her hiding spot in the front of the office.

Four esse's kicked the front door in and made their way to Taz's office.

Taz sat behind his desk as they walked into his office with their guns trained on him.

"Looks like we caught you with your pants down," the first one through the door said in broken English.

Taz never understood why people did this. If you were supposed to kill someone, go ahead and kill them. There was something about when a person thought they had the upper hand that they tended to let their guard down, and that's exactly what they did. What they didn't know was that Taz was only playing the role of sheep. He was getting ready to show them his teeth.

"You could say that. Or maybe I caught you with yours down!" Taz shot back.

"Four guns to one." He gestured around him.

BOOM! BOOM! BOOM! BOOM! BOOM! Kiki opened fire from behind them, killing three of them. When the lead esse turned around, he shot at Kiki. Taz pulled his gun and put one in his knee. Kiki kicked his gun out of his hand as he fell to the ground. Taz walked around the desk and squatted down by his head.

"Looks like you're in a bad spot, homie," Taz said.

Kiki hit him in the head with the butt of her gun, knocking him out.

They loaded all the bodies up and drove to little Haiti and threw the three dead ones out, then went to Kiki's house. They carried the remaining man into the basement and strapped him to a chair. Taz slapped him and woke him up.

"Now how you want to do this? Easy way or the hard way?" Taz asked.

"Fuck you, pendejo," he said and spit in Taz's face.

"You know you fucked up," said Taz, wiping his face.

Taz went and grabbed a pair of vice grips and stood in front of him. He grabbed one of his hands and used the vice grips to rip one of his fingernails off.

"Aaahh!" the man yelled, nearly passing out from the pain.

"Holler all you want. It won't do you no good," Taz said, ripping another nail off.

Taz ripped off all the nails on his right hand as he continued to scream his lungs out

"Where do y'all have the little boy at?" Kiki asked, but he continued to just stare at her.

Taz walked up the stairs and came back with a glass of saltwater. He poured a little on his hand and watched him writhe and yell in pain.

Taz waited a few minutes and was about to pour some more of the saltwater on his fingers when he screamed, "Okay, okay, I'll tell you! He's in a house. It's 1649 Webster Avenue!"

Kiki shot him and they put him in her truck. They drove to a swamp and tossed him in. Then Kiki drove to the address he'd given them and drove by. It was a two-story house in an okay neighborhood so they were going to have to play it safe because they didn't need any police interference. Kiki parked on the street directly behind the house and they got out.

Taz checked the clip to his baby nine and crept up to the back of the house. He peeked in the kitchen window and saw two esse's at the table and another one in the living room. There was no telling how many more were in the house.

"A car just pulled up out front," Kiki whispered. "Domino's. It's a pizza."

This was going to be their chance. They were going to have to use some finesse. They walked to the side of the house and peeked inside. There was an empty bedroom. Taz checked the window and it was open. He lifted Kiki up into it, then he climbed in behind her.

"Our first priority is Keishawn," he said into Kiki's ear.

Kiki cracked the door and peeked into the hallway. They heard a bunch of talking towards the front, so they were probably in the kitchen eating.

"You go that way and I'm going that way," Taz said.

They crept off in search of Keishawn. Taz walked up the steps to the second floor. The first room he got to was also empty, but when he looked in the next one, he saw Keishawn balled up on a little cat. He rushed into the room and grabbed him up.

"Keishawn, you remember me?" Taz asked and he nodded his head. "I'm going to get you out of here, but you have to be quiet."

Taz picked him up and was making his way down the steps when he heard shots then rapid Spanish being spoken.

"Shit!" Taz said, rushing Keishawn down the stairs and into the room where they came through the window. "Wait right here. I'll be right back."

Taz went to help Kiki. There were five more shots in the front of the house, then Kiki said, "It's all good. Now let's go before the police get here."

They got Keishawn out of the house and back to Mary unscathed. Kiki wanted to kill Mary, but Taz explained to Kiki that a mother's love was the strongest love there was. Taz did tell Mary that she had to go back to Fayetteville and not to come back to Miami - ever.

Nicholas Lock

Chapter 14

When the Mexican Cartel killed Kiana's husband, they put a major dent in OTF's day-to-day operations. Marvin was the one that handled all the street level operations, so with him gone, everything fell on Kiana's shoulders. The cartel had caught her sons slipping and cut them up and sent her the heads so all Kiana had left was Meosha and Kiki. Kiana acted as if she was good, but Taz could tell losing her husband and her boys was having an effect on her. Meosha wasn't street savvy enough to really be of any assistance and Kiki had made it clear she wanted nothing to do with running OTF.

"Fuck!" Kiana slammed the phone down. "They just hit two more of my spots."

Everybody was crowded in her office: Taz, Kiki, PJ, TK, Reggie, and Meosha. They were discussing the ongoing war with the Mexican Cartel, trying to come up with a solution. Taz was in the back looking at the various pictures Kiana had posted around her office. He was a little uncomfortable being around Kiki and her mom since he'd fucked them both. Who knew what would happen if Kiki found out? Kiki and her mom had already fought one time and he wasn't about to be the reason they fought again.

"Me and Taz are going to hit two more of his warehouses in the coming days, and that should give us a respite from their attacks," Kiki said.

"Good, because we can barely make any money," PJ added.

"Why you not saying nothing?" Meosha questioned Taz, causing everyone to look his way

Taz had to measure his words because he didn't want to crush anyone's hopes and dreams. "The truth of the matter is that no matter what we do, as long as Hector is alive, he's going to keep coming. Hitting his warehouses is the equivalent to bees stinging a bear. It really just pisses him off. You see, every time we hit him, he hits back ten times harder."

"Bella is the key," Kiana stated, making Taz's head snap her way.

"Kiana, choose your next words carefully now," he said and they locked eyes.

Taz could see she wanted to say something, but thought better of it.

This was the first time they had been around each other and he could feel the sexual energy she was putting out in his direction. He hoped Kiki didn't.

"So what do you propose we do?" TK questioned.

"Nothing. Just keep getting that bread. Let me and Kiki handle Hector. Either I'm going to kill him or he's going to kill me. And you, Kiana, you the head of OTF for a reason. Use your head. Change up everything From your trap spots to the place you get your hair done because I'm about to turn the heat all the way up on Hector, and in turn, he's going to turn it up on y'all."

While they were talking, Taz had come up with a plan. Taz was about to make it where it was going to be hard for Hector to keep it hot on them without some of the heat coming back his way.

***

"You know what it do, right?" Taz questioned Kiki.

They were back in Miami getting ready to set Taz's plan in motion.

Taz and Kiki were outside of the warehouse in Miami. The only difference between this one and the one in Houston was that they weren't going to rob it. Instead, they were going to make it hot.

Taz went to the front while Kiki went to the back. Kiki started shooting into the warehouse while Taz waited on someone to run out the front. The door swung open and Taz started shooting the choppa, making whoever that was about to come out think twice. The people that were standing around on the dock started running and screaming, which was just what Taz and Kiki wanted. Taz let the choppa spit a few more times, then took back off towards the car, leaving the docks in chaos. They got into the car just as a cop car came flying past them. They passed five more cop cars on their way to the airport. Their next stop was going to be New York. Their flight was pre-booked, so all they had to do was go in and board the plane.

"Check it out." Kiki passed Taz her phone as they sat down in first class.

There was a news special about one of biggest drug finds in Miami history.

"Hi, this is Nancy Newman for Channel Eleven news and we're outside of a warehouse on the docks in Miami. Police were responding to a shooting call and made a major discovery. They found half a ton of cocaine and three million dollars in cash. There were ten suspects taken into custody. I'm being told that this warehouse belongs to Hector Vasquez, the import/export mogul."

Taz cut it off. He'd seen enough. They'd accomplished the first part of the mission and gotten his name out. Now it was time to make him hot.

"You fucking me tonight." Kiki leaned over into Taz.

"Nah, I'm about to fuck you in a minute. Go to the bathroom and wait for me."

Kiki got up and almost ran to the bathroom. Taz followed behind her a minute later. When he walked in, she already had her pants around her ankles and was bent over the sink. Taz locked the door and just stood there looking at her pink pussy peeking out from between her thick thighs. Taz slapped her ass and watched as it moved like it had water in it.

"Get up on the sink. I want to see your sexy ass as I punish this cat."

Kiki kicked one of her pants legs off and got up on the sink. Taz rubbed his dick up and down her slit, making her bite down on her lip. She looked him in the eyes as she grabbed hold of his wood and put it in.

"Damn, Kiki."

Kiki's pussy was so tight and wet it had him moaning. Taz made her lean back until her head was up against the mirror, then he pushed her legs up with her toes toward the mirror, opening her up. He started off slow stroking, watching his dick glide in and out of her pussy.

"I love youuu," Kiki moaned.

"I love you too." He leaned up and kissed her.

Taz sped his strokes up, causing Kiki's pussy to start talking to him.

Every time Taz pushed into her pussy, it would make a squishy noise. His dick was shiny from Kiki's juices.

"Nut in me, Taz!"

Taz grabbed her ankles and started giving her long, hard, fast strokes. Taz was expecting her to holler, but instead, she was taking the dick.

"That's what I'm talking about." Taz kept his pace up "Shit!" Taz pushed in to the hilt and let his seed spill inside her.

"Come here," Kiki said lazily.

He leaned up and she kissed him, sticking her tongue in his mouth. He broke away and zipped his pants up while Kiki put her pants back on. When they stepped out of the bathroom, the flight attendant gave them a knowing smirk.

Taz got back to his seat and reclined it. He still couldn't believe he and Kiki were fucking on a regular basis. It just felt funny after all the years of calling her his little sister. It was what it was now. He wondered what she would say if she knew he had fucked her mother. He'd deal with it if it ever came up. For now, he was going to grab some rest

When Taz woke up, they were just landing at JFK international Airport.

"Get your ass up." He nudged Kiki.

They walked off the plane hand in hand. They met Vinny at an Italian restaurant called Meatball Palace in Brooklyn and he provided them with the guns they needed.

"How much longer do you think it's going to be before you wrap this up?" asked Vinny.

"Soon enough; soon enough." Taz kept it short.

There was something he didn't like about him, but he couldn't place what it was. It was probably just the fact that they were using Taz and them to get Hector, but Taz was using them as well so it really didn't matter.

"I don't like him." Kiki voiced what Taz was thinking

"Me either, so the sooner we kill Hector, the sooner we can cut ties with him. Now look, you know New York hot as hell. We're going to have to do this and get low ASAP because they're going to swarm the area and I'm NOT going to jail up here," he warned her.

"Let's go."

They found the warehouse in New York in almost the same place as the one in Miami. Hector thought he was smart by posting the cartel members outside. He thought they were still trying to rob him, but that couldn't have been farther from the truth. Hector had actually helped him because now all they had to do was kill a few of the guards and duck off. Taz and Kiki got out of the car and got within about thirty feet and started plucking the guards off one by one. Once again, everyone on the dock started to get low. They were running back to the car when someone behind them yelled, "Freeze!"

Kiki turned around firing, knocking him to his back. They made it to the car and swerved out. Taz was going to say something to her about shooting the police officer, but she read his mind and said, "You said you weren't going to jail up here and I just solidified your statement."

Taz smiled at her and got them to the airport without further incident. They were on the plane back to Miami when his phone rang.

"What's up?"

"So what, you done with me?" Nesha asked. "I know you not going to leave your stanking-ass bitch. I was just in my feelings."

Taz had really fallen back from dealing with Nesha. He didn't have time to be dealing with her while she was on her bullshit, especially if it was going to cause him problems at home.

"I been mad busy."

"Nigga, ya made time fa mi in da past. What's different now?"

Taz knew she was mad because every time she got mad, her accent would get stronger and more pronounced.

"Nesha, I had a long day and I'm on my second flight today. Let me call you when I touch down."

"Yeah, make sure you do dat, 'cause we need to talk."

Taz didn't like the way she said that so he asked, "About what?"

Nesha paused for a minute and said, "I'm pregnant."

Nicholas Lock

Chapter 15

Taz didn't go talk to Nesha immediately. He waited a few days. He had to lay up with Bella and his babies first. Junior was getting so big so fast that Taz didn't want to miss one moment. Plus he hadn't figured out how to play the situation with Nesha saying she was pregnant. If Bella found out, it was going to be World War III in his house.

"Where you going?" Bella asked. She had gotten used to him being at the house.

"I got to handle some business. I'll be back later." He kissed her on the forehead.

As Taz was walking out of his house, Kiki was walking out of hers.

"Where you going with them little-ass shorts on?" Taz asked.

Kiki was wearing some green boy shorts and a wife beater that was cut in half, showing off her flat stomach.

"I'm going to get me something to eat, damn! Unless you're going to come feed me that dick."

"Kiki, you know you can't suck no dick." Taz laughed.

"Practice makes perfect." She licked her lips.

"If I didn't have nothing to do, I'd probably take you up on that. Go get your food and get your ass back home with them clothes on," he said and took off to Nesha's house.

Taz went by her house but she wasn't there, so he went on campus to look for her. Every time he would call her, she would ignore his calls. He went through the whole campus and couldn't find her. He was going to try the cafeteria, then he was going back home. *Damn!* he thought to himself, *the cafeteria is live!* Everywhere he looked, he saw bad hoes. "I should've took my ass to college," he said out loud.

He scanned the cafeteria looking for Nesha, then he spotted her red dreads. She was in a crowd of people looking good as hell. She had on some white and blue Chanel capris, a white Chanel collar shirt, and some white and blue Chanel sneakers. Taz's temper went all the way through the roof when he saw a dude lean down and whisper in her ear. She waved him off, but Taz still didn't like it. Taz came up behind her and slapped her on the ass. She spun around and was about to snap until she saw Taz. Nesha rolled her eyes about twenty times and turned back around.

"Hey, keep your hands off her," the dude that had whispered in her ear said.

Taz looked at him and wrapped his arms around Nesha's waist.

"Get the hell off me!" She tried to wiggle free, but Taz held her tighter.

"Let her go!" The dude pushed Taz.

Taz laughed the push off because there wasn't a doubt in his mind that the boy couldn't do a thing with him.

"This your dude or something?" Taz asked Nesha and she just stared at him. "Say no more."

Taz was done with that. He started walking out when a short, petite chick grabbed his arm.

"You go here?" she asked.

"Nah, ma, but I'm going to catch up to you." He tried walking away, but she still had his arm.

"Take my number," she told him.

"Bitch, if you don't take your hand off of him." Nesha walked up and got in the girl's face.

Taz walked off while they argued back and forth. He got to his car and was about to pull off when Nesha tapped on his passenger side window.

"Yeah." He cracked the window.

"Really?"

"Talk before I pull off."

"So that's how you treat your child's mother?"

"Nah, that's your boyfriend's baby." Taz was about to pull off, but she stuck her arm in the window and unlocked the door, then climbed in.

"He's not my boyfriend! He's just somebody that always be trying to get with me. Thank you very much. And the only person I've been fucking is you so DON'T try to play me. Now take me home." She folded her arms.

Taz sat there looking at her a few minutes before pulling off. They didn't say anything to each other on the ride to her house.

"What are we going to do?" Taz asked when they walked into her apartment.

"What are you asking me?" Nesha scrunched her face up.

"Are you keeping it?"

"Yes!" she screamed.

"A'ight. I need me another boy anyway."

He caught her off-guard. She was expecting him to be upset, but Taz didn't cry over spilled milk.

"Not a boy, but a girl. And this is what I got planned. I want to make the extra room a nursery. Then I seen this crib at Babies R Us——"

"Hold up, hold up," Taz said, seeing Hector's face on the news. "Turn that up."

"Breaking news! The FBI and DEA have issued a warrant of arrest for Hector Vasquez, the billionaire import/export businessman. The government passed down a twenty count indictment earlier today. Mr. Vasquez has fled the country and is believed to be back in his home country of Mexico."

Taz cut the TV off. This was good and bad. It was good because now they'd be able to focus their efforts on one spot.

It was bad because now Hector could throw caution to the wind and give them his full attention. The time for them to strike was now. They needed to take full advantage of Hector's misfortune before he could regroup.

Taz sat back listening to Nesha and her plans for the baby while he made plans in his head to kill Hector.

Chapter 16

"What's taking so long?" Vinnie asked Taz.

It had been four months since Hector had gone on the run and they still couldn't catch up to him. The Mafia - or at least Vinnie - was getting restless because Taz still hadn't killed Hector. It wasn't for a lack of trying. They hadn't seen any of the Mexican Cartel's people whatsoever, which worried Taz. Everyone else felt like it was over because Hector was dealing with all his legal woes, but Taz wasn't going for it. He tried to explain to them that Hector didn't raise through the ranks of the cartel by being vicious; he did it with his brain. While everyone else was playing checkers, Hector was playing chess. No way was Hector going to let Juan's murder go unpunished.

"We can't pinpoint a definite location for him. Maybe you could assist with that since you're not doing shit else." Taz began to get hot

"I'll see what I can do," he said and hung up.

"Stop!" Taz yelled, trying to keep Junior from putting his keys in his mouth.

Since Hector had gone on the run, Isabella had all but cut him off. Taz was waiting on the right time to try to get the location of Hector's hideout spot in Mexico from her.

"Bae I'm about to go by the Wiener Works office. You want something to eat? D'Azia, Neveah, y'all want something?

"Bring me a footlong and some chili cheese fries," Bella said.

"We want a strawberry milkshake!"

"It's winter time and y'all want ice cream." He shook his head.

He put Junior in his car seat and put him in the G-wagon. Ever since Taz had learned the G-wagon was bulletproof, he'd all but claimed it as his own. Bella didn't too much care because Taz had been spending a lot of time around the house. He'd duck off and go chill with Quanesha every so often. She'd recently found out she was having a boy. Every time he talked to her, she had a new name she wanted his opinion on.

Kiki was still being Kiki. Taz had gotten her to start merging into the legal side of things. He gave her a spot in his real estate business and she opened a beauty shop on the South Beach strip that was already turning over a profit. Life was good. They just needed to kill Hector. TK, PJ, and Reggie were even trying their hands at some legit ventures. TK got himself a landscaping business. PJ got a barbershop and Reggie had a paint and body shop.

"Aww, he's so cute," Victoria said when Taz walked in with Junior in his arms. "Oh, and guess what?"

"What?" He sat down on the sofa in her office.

"My divorce was finalized yesterday, so you owe me a celebration party," she reminded him.

"I got you. I'm going to get you right,"

"Aww, he wants me," she said, seeing Junior reaching for her.

"Nah, he seeing them big-ass titties."

"Hush," said Victoria, grabbing Junior from Taz. "Oh my goodness," she said as Junior immediately reached for her breasts.

"I told you. His mama's breasts feeding him, so he think all titties mean food."

Taz got up and walked behind her and grabbed her butt. She tried to swat his hand away, but she had to keep a hand on Junior.

"You going to let me and my son run a train on you?" Taz slid up on her.

"Stop being naughty, D'angelo!"

Taz pulled one of her breasts out and Junior immediately latched on, trying to suck some milk out.

"Ehh!" Junior made the noise when he didn't get any milk, causing both of them to laugh.

Taz gave her one of his bottles and she started feeding him. Taz left Junior with Victoria while he went down the road to get Bella and his girls their food. When he got back, Junior was asleep across Victoria's lap while she typed on her laptop. Taz grabbed him and motioned to her that he was going to call her.

When Taz pulled back up to his house, he saw Kiki outside on her phone waving her hands around animatedly.

"Your godmama crazy as hell," Taz told his sleeping son.

Taz knew something wasn't right when he got a better look at her face. She was crying.

"What's wrong with you?"

She jumped when Taz asked her the question. She was so into the phone call that she hadn't even seen him when he pulled up. She ran into his arms crying, waking Junior up.

"They killed all of them!" she wailed.

"Who?"

"TK, PJ, and Reggie," Kiki said, dealing him a blow akin to the one Gutta had dealt him when he killed his baby sister.

***

Taz didn't go to the funerals. He couldn't handle seeing his niggas laid up in caskets. He'd paid for all their services and gave their mothers some money. Taz hadn't left the house but one time since he'd gotten the news. Taz had told everybody not to get too comfortable, but obviously they didn't listen. They'd allowed themselves to get caught slipping in a major way. They were sitting outside in the projects on the west side of Atlanta fucking with some bitches when some esse's pulled up and gunned them down. Taz was in his bedroom going over everything in his mind when something popped into his mind. He called Kiki who was still in Atlanta.

"Hello?"

"Yo, who else died that night?"

"Just them, why?"

"Go and round them hoes up and I'll be there in a few hours." Taz hung up.

"Where you going, baby?" Bella asked, seeing Taz getting dressed, but he ignored her.

Taz hadn't said two words to her since he'd gotten the news. Her daddy was the reason he'd just buried three of his niggas that he had a lot of love for. Taz had been debating leaving her alone and getting a house with Nesha, but he didn't want to make a rash decision, especially while he was in his feelings. Isabella knew Taz was feeling a certain kind of way because she was doing everything in her power to get in his good graces.

Taz got his bag, kissed his babies, and walked out without saying anything to Bella. He drove the whole way to Atlanta nonstop. He got to Atlanta at one o'clock in the morning.

"Where you at?" he asked Kiki, and she gave him directions.

Taz pulled up in Bankhead, parked in front of an older house, and got out. Kiki opened the door as soon as his feet touched the steps. Kiki led him to the backroom, where there were four women tied up on the floor.

"Sit them up," he said

Taz bent down and snatched the gags out of their mouths and said, "I'm only going to ask this one time. Who told y'all to set them up?"

Taz had come to the conclusion that they had set TK and them up. At least one of them knew something. There was no way that they got through that ordeal and didn't get hit one time. The news said the police found a hundred rounds.

"We don't know——"

BOOM! Taz shot her in the face, causing the other girls to scream.

"Now who told y'all to set them up?"

"I don't know! He just told me he'd give us two thousand dollars apiece to get them to the projects!" one of the girls said.

"He was an older baldheaded Mexican dude. He had a tattoo on his face of a skull and crossbones," she told Taz, and that was all he needed to hear

BOOM! BOOM! BOOM! Taz blessed them all with headshots. "Come on," he told Kiki. "We got a serious problem. Do you know who she described?" asked Taz when they got outside.

"Who?"

"He was the Mexican Cartel's hitman before Hector let Juan run everything. He's the one that trained Pablo. His name is Javier, but his hood name is Javier Voorhees because he always wore the hockey mask that Jason wore and his weapon of choice was the machete."

When Taz was doing his research on Hector before dealing with him. Javier's name came up too, only it said he had fell off the grid. Before that, he was their go-to man. If there was a problem that needed to be dealt with or if they just wanted to send a message, he was who they called. His success rate was 100%. He didn't fail, obviously. Hector had called him in to handle him and OTF.

"Fuck him, he bleed too." Kiki worked herself up.

"Facts. But he a different breed, Kiki. Ain't no playing with him, period! Make sure you tell Kiana to up her security because he plays by a different set of rules. Wear your vest at all times," he said and walked off, leaving Kiki in a state of bewilderment.

Chapter 17

"I found out where he is," Vinnie told Taz.

"Where?"

"Pueblo, Mexico. At his compound in the mountains."

"I don't know why you told me that! It's impossible to get to him. I've heard about that spot. He built it at the base of the Volcanae Pico de Orizaba. It would take the U.S. Army to penetrate that place!"

"That's your problem. Solve it!" Vinnie yelled, causing Taz to take the phone away from his ear and look at it.

"Vinnie, Vinnie, Vinnie. I don't know who you think you're talking to, but you might want to reevaluate your actions. I'm the last person in the world you want to offend right now, so what we're going to do is act like this never happened. I'll call you with an update in a few weeks," Taz stated calmly and then hung up.

"Da da." Junior spoke his first words, looking up at Taz

"That's so not fair," Bella said, hearing Junior.

Taz still wasn't talking to her. He wasn't even sleeping in the bed with her. He'd either sleep with Neveah or D'Azia and sometimes he'd go next door, fuck Kiki, and sleep there.

"How long are you going to give me the silent treatment?" she asked and Taz ignored her.

Taz didn't know how long he was going to be at odds with Bella because he hadn't given it any thought. Every time he looked at her, he got mad, because if she would've given her dad up, his boys would still be there.

He put his son in his walker and went to get dressed. Tonight Taz was going to give Victoria her celebration party.

"Taz, I swear to God!" Kiki came busting into his house and into his bedroom.

"No she didn't," Bella said out loud, running to her nightstand to get her .380

CLICK! CLICK! Kiki cocked her .10mm. "Bitch, do it! I'll rearrange your whole face plate with these hollow points," she said, gritting her teeth.

Bella stopped in her tracks. You could hear in Kiki's voice that she was dead serious.

"What's good?" Taz asked, looking into her grey eyes.

"They found Mike and Keon in the trunk of a car chopped up in pieces," she told Taz, tears brimming her eyes. "Bitch, you so close to dying, it don't make sense! Whether you want to believe it or not, you're in this! Smack dab in the middle, and it's going to come a time when you're going to be forced to choose a side. I pray you choose the other side." Kiki stormed out of the house

This was going to cause Taz even more problems. The Mexican Cartel had now killed all of OTF's main members. Taz could read Kiana's mind right now and it involved sending Bella's head to Hector. He wasn't going to try to convince her otherwise because it would be futile. If Taz was in her shoes, he'd do the same thing. It was what it was now. He'd already made it clear if they harmed one hair on Bella's head, it was smoke. He didn't give a fuck, and Kiana also knew that no matter the situation, Kiki wasn't going to go against Taz.

***

"Liv, my feet are killing me," Victoria said, walking into her house.

Victoria was just getting off work and couldn't wait to take a bath and curl up with a glass of wine.

"Okay, I'll talk to you tomorrow." She hung up and walked up the steps to her bedroom "Oh my God!" Victoria gasped. Taz was sitting on the edge of her bed, naked with a rock hard dick.

"You wanted a celebration, so tonight is your celebration night."

Taz walked up to her, picked her up, and sat her on the bed. Victoria didn't resist. She let Taz have his way. He pulled her bun out, letting her hair fall. Taz started sucking on her neck, leaving hickies all over her neck.

"Taz," Victoria moaned, rubbing her thighs together in anticipation of the dick she was about to get.

Taz took her blouse off and sucked one of her erect nipples into his mouth while undoing her shirt.

"Bite my titties!" she screamed, and Taz nibbled on her nipple, causing her to rock back and forth like she was riding his dick.

Taz kissed his way down her stomach until he got between her legs. Her red thong was soaking wet. He could smell her pussy through the thong.

"Why this pussy so wet?" Taz asked, sliding her thong off.

She crossed her ankles around his neck and pulled him to her pussy.

Taz pecked around her pussy lips, but he didn't touch her clit. Victoria tried to lift her hips to get his tongue on her clit, but he'd move every time she got close.

"Stop teasing me," she whined.

Taz stuck two fingers inside her pussy and flicked his tongue across her clit, making her jump. Victoria grabbed two handfuls of his dreads and rode his tongue until she gushed all over his face. Taz got up and grabbed a bottle of syrup off the headboard and coated his dick in it. He pulled her to the edge of the bed and she took over from there. Victoria licked around the head, sucking the syrup off the tip. Then she took his dick all the way to the back of her throat and massaged his balls with her hand.

"That's right, suck this dick! You like sucking my dick, don't you?" Taz asked, running his hands through her hair.

"Yeah! I love it! I'm your slut now." She slapped her tongue with his dick.

Taz grabbed the sides of her face and pumped her mouth like it was a pussy. She relaxed her throat muscles as Taz slid his pipe back and forth down her throat. Victoria had sucked all the syrup off his dick and wanted more.

"You better not miss a drop," Taz told Victoria as he emptied his nuts into her mouth.

She swallowed and Taz pushed her into the middle of the bed and climbed between her legs.

"You better fuck this pussy good. I've been waiting on this since that night at my house," Victoria said as he lined his dick up with her wet opening.

"Damn, Vicky." Taz pushed into her and almost busted his nut. Her pussy was a fool! "Get on top." Taz knew if he stayed on top, he'd nut.

Victoria got on top and started bucking her hips like she was in a bull riding contest.

"Suck my titties." Victoria leaned down so Taz could suck on her double D's.

He alternated between her breasts while gripping her ass, forcing her to go all the way down on his dick.

"Turn around," Taz told her and she turned around with his dick still in her. While she bounced up and down on his dick, Taz stuck his finger in her butt, making her go crazy. Victoria did a split and leaned up and was pushing back on his dick using her hands.

"Yeah, do that shit right there," Taz said.

Taz let Victoria ride his dick in reverse cowgirl a few more minutes before making her get up.

"What's the matter?"

"You know what time it is. Assume the position."

Victoria smiled and got on her hands and knees. He pushed back into her dripping pussy, getting his dick wet, then pulled out and pushed the head of his dick into her butt.

"Oh God!" she screamed as he worked into her.

Taz let her adjust and relax, then he pounded her guts out. Taz was slamming into her so hard the mattress was coming off the bed.

"You like the way I take this dick, don't you?" Victoria threw her ass back.

Taz grabbed her hips and went into overdrive. She tried to match his strokes, but Taz was going too hard

"I'm taking this diiiick!" she hollered as Taz continued to mash her out.

"Whose bitch is you?"

"Yours, Taz! Yours!"

Taz spilled his kids inside her ass and lay back on the bed spent.

Victoria went in the bathroom, cleaned up, then came out with a soapy rag and cleaned Taz off. Taz dozed off with Victoria curled up beside him.

Nicholas Lock

Chapter 18

Once again, everything had been quiet. It had been another four months since anything had happened, but this was just the quiet before the storm. No more being on defense. They were about to go on offense. Taz and Kiki had been gathering intel on all the Mexican Cartel's operations in the U.S. Taz had a lot of free time on his hands. Taz wanted to have everything wrapped up by then. They wanted smoke, and that's what Taz and Kiki were going to give them. Every stronghold the Mexican Cartel had was about to feel the heat. Javier had yet to show his face but Taz was waiting. His next big engagements would be Nesha having his son, which was next month, then Junior's first birthday was the month after.

Taz was wrapping his work up at his real estate business when Keishana walked in his office and sat down.

"What you about to get into?" she asked.

"Nothing really, why?"

"I know you, Taz, stop lying to me."

"I'm about to make somebody's mama cry. They killed Kiki's dad and all her brothers, then they killed TK, PJ, and Reggie, so you already know what time it is."

Keishana couldn't say much after that. "Please be safe. I don't want nothing to happen to you," she confessed

"I'm always safe." He lifted his shirt, showing Keishana his bulletproof vest.

"You better be. And who was that pregnant girl I seen you with at the mall?"

"Damn, nosy." He smiled "That's just this college chick I got pregnant, why?"

"Nothing really. I just thought you looked cute together and she looked familiar. Do I know her?"

"Nah, she used to go to Fayetteville State though. So you probably seen her in the city," Taz informed her.

"Yeah, most likely. Well, I'm about to go show a house. I'll see you later on." She walked out.

"Nigga, come on! The flight leaves in thirty minutes." Kiki rushed into his office.

Taz and Kiki were catching a flight to Brownsville, Texas. It was one of the strongholds Taz had found out about while digging for information on Hector and his cartel. The Mexican Cartel ran the entire city and with Brownsville sitting on the border of Texas and Mexico, their population was more than half Hispanic. Taz and Kiki were about to shoot the murder rate of Brownsville through the roof.

They got to the airport and onto the plane with minutes to spare. Taz slept the whole flight. He was going to need his rest for all the mayhem he had planned.

Kiki rented a house on the northside of Brownsville so they didn't have to worry about drawing any heat at a hotel. Kiki was trying to get some get-back for all the male members in her immediate family getting killed while Taz was trying to flush Javier out. There was going to be no finesse to what they were about to do. Taz and Kiki were going to go to an all Hispanic hood and kill everyone that had either an M tattooed under their right eye with a crown over it or a bald head with the horns tattooed in the front. Both were symbols of Mexican Cartel membership.

"No kids and no women," said Taz as he loaded the drum on an AK-47.

"No women? Kiki looked up from loading her street sweeper. "I'm a woman and I'll kill you faster than a nigga will." She made a very valid point.

"But you're not the average woman either, Kiki." Taz remembered the time she had told Meosha that Meosha got wet from laying on her back while she got wet from putting niggas on they backs.

"Anyway." Kiki went back to loading the street sweeper

Once again, Kiana had come through with weapons galore. They had guns on top of guns! Taz kept it simple by snatching up one of the choppas while Kiki, being extra as usual, grabbed the automatic shotgun. They both donned level four military vests and Taz snatched up a few flash grenades.

"I'm driving." Taz grabbed the keys to the Camaro rental before Kiki could.

They drove across town to one of the neighborhoods that the Mexican Cartel dominated. It was nine-thirty at night and the block was jumping! You could tell that they weren't worried about the police because they were selling work out in the open like it was legal. There were crackheads and prostitutes everywhere. Taz looked around and saw cartel members standing around in different positions. At first look they seemed to be just randomly standing around, but Taz noticed they were in strategic positions and in the middle was a house that looked like it had been recently remodeled.

"I'm about to squeeze." Kiki started to roll her window down.

"No! No. No. Something not right. Look how they're standing around the block. It's something special about that house and we're going to find out what it is."

Taz drove to the end of the street, hoping it was going to be a street he could turn on to be behind the house, but it was only woods. Taz backed the car up to the woods and cut the car off.

"Go ahead and get that thought out of your head. I'm not going into them woods," Kiki told Taz.

"Not big bad Kiki! I know you not scared of no woods," he teased.

"Nigga, it's probably snakes, bears, and all kinds of creepy shit in them woods."

"Suck it up. Let's get to it."

The got out and walked into the wood line.

"Get your scary ass off me!" Taz told Kiki. She had the street sweeper in one hand and Taz's thermal shirt in the other.

They got to the back of the desired house without incident and just as Taz expected, there was no one in the back of the house.

"We don't know what or who is in this house, so expect the unexpected," said Taz.

They crept up to the back of the house and Taz kicked the door in. They entered the house ready to shoot, but they didn't have a target.

"You hear that?" Kiki whispered.

There were screams coming from the back of the house, which was why nobody heard the door. Taz and Kiki moved through the house and the screams got louder as they moved down the hallway.

"Please, no!" someone begged.

Taz and Kiki burst into the room where the screams were coming from and Taz slipped and fell on the floor. Taz looked up and was looking into the face of a hockey mask. Javier had his machete in his hand but before he could move in Taz's direction, Kiki hit him in the chest with the street sweeper, knocking him through the window. When Taz looked to see what he'd slipped in, he noticed he was covered in blood. He looked around the room and saw blood everywhere, then he saw why. There was a dude chained up in the corner. Javier had chopped him up! One of his legs was gone from the knees down and one of his arms was barely hanging on.

"Get your ass up!" Kiki yelled as the esse's outside started sending shots inside the house.

BOOM! BOOM! BOOM! BOOM! Kiki started shooting the street sweeper. Taz hopped up and ran back to the back door. They had to get out of there because if they let them trap them in the house, they were a done deal. Taz and Kiki ran out the back just as two esse's came around the house. BOOM! BOOM! KAH! KAH! KAH! Taz hit one and Kiki dropped the other on. They hit the wood line and rushed to the Camaro, then swerved off.

"I got him!" Kiki yelled excitedly, talking about hitting Javier in the chest.

"No you didn't," Taz said in awe as they passed Javier on the side of the road waving his machete their way.

"Turn around!" she yelled.

"Kiki, that'd be a death sentence to go back. Chill, we're going to get him. We got all week! We're going back to the spot. I'm going to get out these bloody clothes and you about to work on your head game," Taz said, making Kiki lick her lips.

Nicholas Lock

Chapter 19

"Nah, nigga!" Taz yelled, shooting his AR-15.

Taz and Kiki were on the east side of Brownsville giving some more of the Mexican Cartel's people hell. They'd been in Brownsville for three days now and they'd shot or killed over thirty esse's. Javier was missing. There hadn't even been a glimpse of him since their run-in.

TAT! TAT! TAT! TAT! Kiki shot an esse trying to duck behind a car. They were in the middle of the street on some Wild Wild West shit.

"Watch out!" Kiki screamed.

Taz ducked and Kiki shot a girl who had a shotgun trained on Taz.

"No women, huh?" Kiki rolled her eyes, moving on to another target.

"Come on! Come on!" Taz yelled, hearing sirens in the distance.

They got in the car and peeled out. Taz was about to pull onto the street their house was on when a police car got behind them and hit their sirens. Taz and Kiki looked at each other and no words were needed. Taz hit the gas and the Camaro started, leaving the police car. He turned right and put some distance between them and the police car. Taz thought he was home free, then a Charger got behind them with their lights flashing.

"Fuck!" Taz knew it wasn't going to be easy to shake. The Charger had way more horsepower than the Camaro.

He started weaving in and out of traffic. Kiki rolled her window down and started raining bullets on the undercover car. The Charger stopped to avoid the bullets, giving them the opportunity they needed. Taz made a hard left then a sharp right and gunned the engine. He looked in the mirror and saw they were in the clear, so he eased up on the gas.

BOOM! A police cruiser T-boned the Camaro, flipping it in the air. The Camaro flipped three times and landed upside down.

"Kiki, you good?"

"Yeah, my foot stuck."

"I'm about to come get you out."

Taz crawled out of the car and went around to the passenger side. Taz wiped the blood out of his face from a cut above his eye and helped Kiki get her foot loose.

"Watch out!" Kiki said a little too late. The police hit Taz in the head, knocking him to the ground.

The police swarmed the car and put Taz and Kiki in handcuffs. Taz went crazy! The last time he'd gotten put in cuffs he was sent away to prison for twelve to sixteen years. He'd gotten that time cut down to eight years and that was a blessing. Now he was on his way to jail and was probably going to have numerous murder charges.

"Taz, I love you. This on me. You went away the first time and it should've been both of us. I'm going to take the charge," Kiki told him.

"Kiki, shut up," he said as he looked out the window.

"You heard what I said," Kiki added.

Something wasn't right. They weren't headed downtown towards the jail. They were going in the opposite direction. Taz nudged Kiki's arm and motioned for her to look out the window. She immediately caught on, but then Taz looked in the front seat and that's when he saw it. The policeman in the passenger seat had an M with the crown on it behind his ear. They were in a bad spot, but the sad thing about it was that Taz was relieved. He'd rather be dead than in somebody's prison again. Not to say he wasn't going out with a bang, but he knew the odds once again weren't in his favor.

They pulled up to an apartment building with about thirty esse's milling about.

"Get out here!" The police snatched Taz and Kiki out of the back. "You're going to learn about fucking with the Mexican Cartel, fool!"

The police handed them off and pulled off. They were roughly escorted into one of the apartments and put in a room. On the way, Taz noticed the building faced the highway. In the room was a mattress, a blanket, and nothing else. It was clear that somebody had recently slept there. Two esse's came into the room and went straight to Taz.

"You killed my brother, pussy!" one said and started punching him.

Taz's hands were still handcuffed behind his back, so there wasn't anything he could do to ward off the blows. Kiki tried to kick him, but the other esse grabbed her by the hair and slammed her head against the wall, dazing her.

"We got something real special for you, bitch! It's about forty of us and we're all going to have a turn with you," he said, grabbing his dick.

The beating took place for about five minutes before he got tired and walked out, leaving Taz's face bloody and swollen. About five minutes later, an older Mexican woman came into the room with a rag and some ice. She uncuffed Taz and cleaned his face, then set the ice beside him. The whole time she never said a word. She uncuffed Kiki and went back to cleaning his face.

"Who told you to do this?" Taz asked.

"Nobody, now shut up!"

Taz sat there and let her doctor on his face. It crossed his mind to try and take her hostage, but he thought better of it. It wouldn't even matter. They were at a disadvantage right now, but as long as his hands were free, he was good.

"If you were anybody else, I would've left you to rot in here."

"What does who I am have to do with you helping me?" Taz questioned.

"You're Isabella's boyfriend," she said, making Taz really look at her to see if he recognized her.

"And who are you?"

"I'm the aunt that raised her," she revealed, giving Taz a glimmer of hope.

"Why are you risking your life?"

"Risking my life? They won't mess with me no matter what I do. Hector is my big brother. He'd kill them and their entire bloodline. I'm going to help you get out of here, but please don't come back because I won't be here next time," she said, walking out.

"You trust her?" Kiki asked.

"Yeah. Bella told me her aunt raised her. Do you have a better idea? She's the best shot we have at getting out of here alive."

Bella's aunt came back in and motioned for them to follow her. She gave them two hoodies to put on and two pistols. Taz and Kiki put the hoodies on and followed her out of the apartment. They got in a black Blazer and pulled out. She dropped them off at the house Kiki had rented and swerved off. They grabbed their things and called an Uber. They were about to get away from Brownsville as fast as possible. They had dodged death again. Taz didn't think they were going to be able to keep catching lucky breaks. They were going to have to rethink ways to get at the cartel because they could ill afford another slip-up like that again. They'd ducked prison and death all in one day. They were going to need some extra assistance from OTF. OTF had major resources, but just about all of their manpower was focused in Atlanta. Then an idea came to him. He cut his phone on to call Kiana and saw he had a hundred missed calls from Bella. Her aunt must've told her what happened.

"Bella, what's up?"

"Oh my God, I'm so sorry!" she screamed.

"Sorry for what, girl?" Taz was lost.

"I tried! It was too many of them. I killed two of them but they still took them!" she continued to scream and sob into the phone.

"Bella, calm down, what are you talking about?"

"They got Neveah and D'Azia," she said and Taz dropped the phone.

Nicholas Lock

Chapter 20

Taz and Kiki rushed into his house and found Bella on the couch with Junior. Taz snatched her up by her neck and had her on the wall with her feet off the floor.

"Where the fuck are my babies at?" Taz asked, still squeezing her neck

"She can't breathe, Taz," Kiki said, grabbing his arms.

Bella was on the verge of passing out. Taz let her go and she fell to the floor gasping for air. Taz had no compassion right now. His whole reason for living was his daughters. Taz put his girls before any and everything. Bella didn't know it, but she was about two minutes from having a closed casket. He'd told her to make a decision, but she kept bullshitting. If she would've helped Taz a long time ago, this would've never happened. So this was on her, in his eyes, and God forbid if something happened to his babies. Hector was going to get another box, only this time instead of Juan's nuts, it was going to be Bella's head.

"Bitch, where the fuck my babies?"

"I don't know!" she cried.

"That's the wrong answer!" Taz pulled his foot back to kick her and Kiki pushed him.

"Get your shit together! You know she don't know," Kiki defended her.

"You act like I won't put you in a shallow grave right beside her."

"You just mad and in your feelings right now. Focus that energy on finding your daughters. Who took them, Bella?" Kiki asked, helping Bella up off the floor.

"Javier," she said, and all the air rushed out. Taz's lungs felt like he'd gotten punched in the stomach.

The tears started falling from his eyes in buckets. Taz knew that the next time he saw his girls it was probably going to be in a casket. There were so many thoughts running through his mind at the moment, but the one that held the most appeal was killing Bella. If he got his girls back unharmed, he was done! No more streets, no more killing, no more nothing! He had enough money to go retire and live happily ever after. He was going to move to the Virgin Islands and live a quiet, peaceful life. Taz walked out the house because if he stayed any longer, he might kill Bella. He got in his new CT6 and drove around and somehow he ended up at Keishana's house.

"What's wrong, Taz?" she asked when she saw him crying.

"They got my girls," he sobbed.

"Oh God." Keishana hugged him.

"Let me crash here, I can't stand looking at Bella right now."

"Of course. You can stay as long as you want."

"Roll up."

Keishana rolled up a fat blunt of loud and they smoked until Taz had mellowed out a little bit.

"What're you going to do?" Keishana inquired.

"It all depends," he said, rubbing his hand down his face. "If I got my babies back, I'm moving to the Virgin Islands and laying back. But if something happens to them, I'm going to help Trump out because I'm going to smoke every single Mexican I run across. Male, female, kids, it's not going to matter. I'm going to rain down death on the Mexican Cartel like nothing ever seen in this lifetime," Taz said, meaning every word he spoke.

Keishana could only shake her head because she knew Taz wasn't playing. She was going to pray that his daughters made it home safely. Then she was going to pray ahead of time for all the families that were going to have to bury their loved ones if something happened to Taz's daughters.

***

It had been a week since Javier had snatched his girls and there hadn't been a word on their condition. Taz hadn't been going out. He'd just been laying in Keishana's bed all the time. It had gotten so bad that Keishana had to call Kiki over

"Nigga, you need to tighten up!" Kiki snatched the covers back.

"Go the fuck on." Taz pulled the covers back up.

Kiki had never seen her brother down this bad. It was tearing her up to see him like this. She couldn't take it. Then her hormones were all over the place, which was making it worse. Kiki had talked to Bella and Bella was trying to get her dad to get the girls back, but he wasn't budging. There were a lot of lives riding on Taz getting his babies back, and that included Bella's. Because if not, Kiki couldn't see Taz saving her anymore.

"What're we going to do, girl?" Keishana asked.

"What can we do but wait and see what happens," said Kiki, plopping down on the sofa.

"Girl, you getting fat too."

"Not fat. I'm just pregnant as hell," Kiki confessed.

"What? By who?" Keishana wanted to know so she could tell Taz

Kiki gave her the look like quit playing. "You know I don't fuck nobody but Taz."

"Gotdamn! That nigga got super sperm! How long y'all been fucking? Because I didn't know. And how far along are you?" Keishana wanted all the details.

"We been fucking for a minute now and I have no idea. I missed my cycle a few times so I'm probably three months," Kiki said, looking down at her stomach.

"No way, you further along than that from the looks of your stomach. That or you got more than one baby in your stomach."

"Don't say that."

"Wait a minute, do Taz know?" asked Keishana.

"No, and you better not tell him. If he finds out, he going to get on some shit. He already overprotective as hell." Kiki rubbed her belly.

"Are you going to keep it?"

Kiki shrugged her shoulders.

"If you kill that boy's baby, OMG! It's already about to be World War III, but if he found that out, it's going to be World War IV, V, and VI." She laughed.

"You stupid." Kiki threw one of the pillows on the couch at her.

"Glad to see everybody's in a good mood," Taz said, walking into the room and out the door, leaving Keishana and Kiki staring at each other.

Taz got in his whip and burnt out. He had to go check on Nesha real quick. He'd been laid up at Keishana's house for the last week but after he checked on Nesha, he was going back to Keishana's spot to lay up some more. He had talked to Bella and she begged him to come home, but he'd refused. He wasn't in the right mindset to be around her. He had calmed down since his initial response to her when he came home. He loved her, and there was no doubt about that she was his baby, but he needed some more time.

"Hey, baby daddy!" Nesha said when she saw Taz.

"What's up, sexy?"

"Nothing. Are you okay, boo? I heard about what happened." She rubbed his back.

"Yeah, I'm good. You ready to have my son?" Taz asked, lifting her sundress up so he could see her big-ass stomach.

"Yes! Ares has to go."

"Ares?"

"That's his name. He was the Greek God of war," she said in a way that dared him to say something.

"Whatever. Grab this." Taz held his Glock .23 out.

"Why? For what?" She acted scared,

"'Cause I said so. Now here." He made her take it

Taz took her to the bedroom and opened the balcony door. He pulled her out on the balcony and got behind her.

"Now look I'm not going to be around you 24/7, so I need to know that you can protect yourself," Taz told her, taking her hands into his. "This is the safety. This is how you cock it. Now all you have to do is aim and shoot. Squeeze the grip tighter. You see that red dot?" She nodded her head. "Whatever that dot is on is what the bullet will hit." Taz gave her a quick lesson on how to use a gun.

"If you stayed with me, I'd be protected," she said naïvely.

"Nah, you'd probably be worse off." He sat on the edge of the bed.

"You know I should be having Ares in about thirteen days. You're going to be there, right?" Nesha sat in his lap facing him.

"Hopefully."

"The doctor told me sex can induce labor." She lifted her sundress over her head. She pulled his dick out and sat on it. Taz lay back and let her ride his dick until she came. Then she got on her knees and sucked him off until he squirted down her throat. They laid down in the bed until she dozed off, then Taz snuck out.

Taz stopped at a CVS pharmacy on his way back to Keishana's house. He had to get some condoms because he couldn't keep getting girls pregnant - at least not until he had his life in order and all his beef was over with.

The house was quiet when he walked in. He knew Keishana always went to bed early. When Taz walked in the bedroom, his breath got caught in his throat. Keishana was naked on top of the covers with her ass propped up. He walked over to the side of the bed to cut the lamp off and let her sleep, but said fuck it. Taz wondered how it was that her ass was up in the air like that, then he saw she had two pillows under her. He usually slept in the bed with her, but she was taking up most of the bed. Taz was walking out of the room, but he had to get one last look at her fat ass and pussy. Taz walked back over to the bed, looking at the way her pussy was poked out, and his dick started to rise.

"Fuck it," Taz said as he reached in his pocket and pulled out one of the gold packs. Taz stripped naked and slid the condom down his dick. "God, please don't let this condom break," he said as he approached Keishana.

Taz rubbed her ass and lined himself up with her pussy. He spit on his hand and rubbed it on the tip of the condom. Taz grabbed her hip with one hand and used the other to guide his dick in.

"Ohhh Goood!" Keishana moaned, waking up immediately

Taz started stroking her pussy, making her clench the sheets, then she came to her senses because she rolled up and stood up.

"Are you fucking stupid, nigga?" She was so mad her black ass was turning red. "I knew you was suicidal, but damn! Your dumb ass want to die slow!" Keishana paced back and forth.

"I got a condom on, girl, shut up and come here."

"What if it breaks, dumbass?"

"Trojans don't break like that. Now come here." Taz was thirsty for her tight pussy. Keishana hadn't been fucked since he had sent her to fuck Zion to give him AIDS, and that had been about three years ago. "Let me get this nut off," he tried again.

"Bring your stupid ass here!" Keishana said, sitting on the edge of the bed.

Taz walked over to her and she checked the condom before taking him down her throat.

"Hell yeah!" Other than Victoria, Keishana's head game was the best. He knew this from before she got AIDS.

It didn't take five minutes before he was filling the condom with his kids. Taz snatched the condom off and was about to go flush it when she said, "Let me taste it."

"Huh?" Taz was lost.

Keishana grabbed the condom out of his hand and dumped the nut into her mouth, swallowing it all.

"Oh yes, you a fool!"

Keishana smirked, walking out of the room while Taz got in the bed and fell right to sleep. She had sucked him to sleep.

Nicholas Lock

Chapter 21

Taz had been doing everything in his power to keep his mind off his daughters. He was still hopeful, but in the back of his mind he was sure they were dead

"What up, Nesha?" Taz answered his phone

"My water just broke!"

"I'm on my way."

Taz got to Nesha's house and helped her into the car. They got to the hospital and Nesha was rushed to the delivery room. Taz put on some scrubs and watched as the doctor prepped

"Aaahh!" Nesha screamed as a contraction hit her. "Mi gon' fuck you up!" she said, seeing the smirk on Taz's face. She was steaming hot.

"Bae, calm down and push my little man out." Taz tried to pacify her.

She rolled her eyes and Taz used a damp rag to wipe the sweat off her face. Taz walked to the end of the bed and peeked over. Her pussy was all the way open. Every time Taz witnessed a birth, he just couldn't understand how a woman would be screaming "it's too much" while having sex, but their pussy opened almost a foot wide.

"Ya supposed to be up here wit mi, not down there staring at mi coochie."

Taz went back to the top of the bed and let Nesha squeeze his hand as she pushed.

"I can see the head, keep pushing." the doctor said.

Nesha was only in labor for a cool eight hours. Taz's son Ares came out like a gangsta. He wasn't crying or anything. He was a big baby. He weighed ten pounds and was just about two feet long at twenty-two inches. You could already tell he was going to be tall. Taz was 6'2" and Nesha was almost six feet herself, so it was a forgone conclusion that Ares was going to have plenty of height. Just like all his other kids, Ares looked just like him except he was high yellow like his mama and had her fire red hair.

"That's why it hurt so much. Look at my baby big-ass head," Nesha said, cuddling him.

"Watch your mouth, and you not about to be making my baby soft either." Nesha looked at him and rolled her eyes, continuing to hug and kiss him.

Taz shook his head. He remembered when Neveah and D'Azia were born and he started to tear up. The nurses took Ares to the nursery and wheeled Nesha to her room.

"He's so pretty," Nesha said, barely able to keep her eyes open.

"Get some rest, bae." He kissed her and walked to the nursery to watch his son.

He watched Ares sleep for about fifteen minutes, then decided to go by Majestic and see what Kiki and Keishana had going on. He pulled into the lot and saw Keishana's car and Kiki's new eight series Beamer. It seemed like she bought a car every other week.

"You need to hit the gym. You getting fat," Taz said, pinching her stomach.

Kiki punched him in the chest. "I'm not fat either!"

"If you say so. What up, Keishana?"

"Shit, just waiting."

Since the night that Taz had tried to fuck Keishana, she had been somewhat avoiding him. Taz was going to address the situation tonight.

"I don't know why you just don't tell him."

"Tell me what?" Taz inquired.

"Nothing," Kiki said quickly, cutting her eyes at Keishana.

He shook his head and walked into his office and saw a package sitting on his desk

"Where this come from?" Taz yelled.

"What?" Kiki asked and froze when she walked in and saw the package on his desk.

"That came yesterday," Keishana said

"Open it, Kiki," Taz told her, turning his back and looking out the window at the sun in the sky.

Taz heard her open the package and then he heard some plastic rustling.

He wanted to turn around, but he couldn't do it. Kiki came up behind him wrapped her arms around his waist and put her head in the middle of his back. Taz tried to turn around and walk over to the package, but Kiki held him tighter.

"Kiki, let me go now."

She let him go and he turned around and saw Keishana crying.

Taz slow-walked to his desk. Taz looked in the package and slumped down in his seat as the tears started to flow. When he caught Javier, he was going to kill him so slow that the devil was going to feel sorry for him. Javier had killed his babies and sent Taz the skin off their faces.

"Aaaahhhh!" he yelled and rushed out the building

He couldn't take it. There was no point in him living. They had killed his reason for waking up every day. Taz reached under the seat of his car and grabbed his hammer. He put the gun to his head and was getting ready to pull the trigger when Kiki walked up.

"So you're going to be selfish like that? You're going to take the easy way out? You just going to leave us?"

"Y'all are going to be good," he said with the gun still to his head

"What about the babies? They're not going to know their daddy."

"Nesha and Bella will see to it they know who their daddy is."

"What about ours?" She started to cry. "I can't raise no baby without you. Yeah, I'm pregnant," Kiki told him, making him put the gun in his lap.

"Quit playing."

"I'm dead serious. I'm probably about two or three months"

Taz shook his head. He had too much on his plate as it was. Now Kiki was saying she was pregnant. He didn't even know if he was going to be alive in the next couple of months because Taz was about to go kamikaze. He was going to hunt Javier and Hector down no matter where they were at. *Oh my God*, he thought. When Bella found out Kiki was pregnant whew! That was going to be a bad situation, but it was over and done with now. He was focused on finding Javier.

***

"Baby, where you at?" Nesha asked.

"I'm in New York. I'll be back in a few days."

Taz was in Brooklyn again meeting Vinnie at the Meatball Palace. Taz needed some information and he was pretty sure Vinnie could help.

"I'm sorry about your girls," Vinnie said when Taz sat down.

"I need you to help me find out where Javier is." Taz wasted no time in asking for what he needed

"It might take a few days because I have to do a lot of reaching out. But I'm pretty sure I can help you." Vinnie made his day.

"I'll be here in New York so the minute you get word, call me."

They shook hands and Taz walked out. Since he was probably going to be in New York for a couple of days, he was going to check the city out. He'd been wanting to check Dyckman Park out for a while.

Taz went back to his hotel room and changed into some white cargo shorts, a white T-shirt and a pair of white low top Air Force 1's. His dreads were now all the way down his back. He had them French braided because it was too hot to have them down. Taz popped the grill in he'd had custom made with Neveah's name across the top and D'Azia's across the bottom in pink and white diamonds. He put on his black and white diamond chain and his Daytona Rolex. He put his .40 in the small of his back and walked out.

When he pulled up to the park, he noticed it was super crowded. Taz had to park down the block and walk the rest of the way. When he got in, he saw why it was so crowded. They were having the *Slam* magazine summer classic. Taz made it just in time for the slam dunk contest. He found a seat in the bleachers a row in front of the top. Everywhere Taz looked, there were hoes and they barely had any clothes on. Taz tuned into the dunk contest just as a young boy did a between the legs 360° windmill dunk. The crowd went bananas!

"Girl, that nigga going to the NBA," a chick behind him said.

Taz turned to see who had said it and saw a group of chicks sitting on the row behind him. They weren't blood raw, but they weren't smack either.

"What you looking at?" one girl asked.

Taz smiled and turned back around to watch the game.

"Damn, nigga, what you got in your mouth?" another one asked.

Taz ignored them and kept watching the dunk contest

"You hear me?" She caused Taz to turn around by pulling one of his braids.

"Yo, shawty, don't touch me," he warned.

"Damn, country boy, where you from? I know you not from around here with that country twang, plus I ain't never seen you before."

Taz looked at the girl that was talking. She looked to be Asian, but she had blue eyes.

"I'm from North Carolina. Now fall back." He turned back around.

"And who you think you is, my daddy?"

Taz could already tell he wasn't going to be able to enjoy the contest, so he got up. He was going to leave before he blanked out. His patience was at zero. He had too much going on in his mind to deal with a slick-mouthed bitch. He got in his rental and swerved off.

Taz was riding through the city when his phone rang.

"What's good, Vinnie?"

"I got some good news and some bad news. The good news is that I found out where Javier is at, but the bad news is that it's going to take a lot of power to get to him."

"Where?"

"Guadalajara, Mexico."

Guadalajara was the biggest city in Mexico and it was the Mexican Cartel's headquarters. It was Brownsville times ten, but Taz could give two fucks! Javier had killed his babies, so he was willing to die trying to get his revenge. He was going to need a little bit of help and he had an idea of just the right person.

Chapter 22

Kiki was trying to fight. Taz was about to go to Bella's hometown of Guadalajara and he wasn't letting her go. Taz wasn't willing to lose anybody else that he loved or cared for. He'd made Bella get in contact with her aunt so she could help him get to Javier.

"So you mean to tell me you're going by yourself?"

"Pretty much," Taz said

"Taz, quit playing with me! You're going to need somebody to watch your back," Kiki pleaded her case

"First off, you're pregnant, and second off, I was doing this shit way before you came into the picture. And maybe you forgot who taught you the game. Now come here."

They shared a kiss, then Taz went to catch his flight. The whole flight Taz reflected on all that had happened in the last few months. He'd lost a whole lot of people he loved. After he dealt with Javier, he was going to deal with Hector once and for all. Taz had come up with a plan that was sure to net Hector. Bella's aunt was waiting for him when he got off the plane.

"You have some big balls, my friend. I despise Javier and that's why I'm helping you, but you do know you're most likely going to die here?" Bella's aunt informed him.

"I don't plan on it. And what do I call you?"

"Just call me Aunt D. I picked up that box and it's in your room already," she said, pulling up outside the hotel. "I'll be back tonight."

Taz walked into the hotel and went straight to his room. He locked the door and went straight to the box. He'd given Kiana a list of things he needed and she'd come through. Taz opened the box and started putting the items on the bed. Taz immediately put the bulletproof vest on. He put the twin Glock

.27's in his shoulder holsters then put extra clips in his pockets.

Taz was loading the SK up when his phone rang. When he saw it was Kiki, he let it go to the voicemail. After getting everything in order, Taz laid back on the bed and pulled his phone out. Taz pulled up the last pictures he'd taken of his daughters and just stared.

"I'm about to get y'all some get-back or die trying," Taz said.

Taz laid there staring at his phone until Aunt D called to tell him she was outside. He grabbed the NV goggles and went out to meet her.

"Look, I'm going to wait for you for fifteen minutes. After that, I'm leaving. Grab him and bring him out so I can take you to the other house and you can do what you need to do," she warned him. She let Taz out down the street from the house Javier was in. Taz walked up the street until he was beside the house. He looked up and shot the grey boxes by the street lights putting the street and the houses in darkness. Taz put the night vision goggles on and walked up to the house. Taz could hear Spanish being spoke inside the house. He knocked the lock off the backdoor and walked in. He was in a kitchen. The night vision goggles had Taz seeing the house as if it was midday instead of the dead of the night. Taz rounded the corner as footsteps started descending the stairs. It was Javier holding a flashlight. Taz put a bullet in his knee, sending him to the ground. Taz hopped on him and tied his hands behind his back.

"Do you know who I am and what I'll do to you?" Javier asked bravely.

"Shut up!"

"Javier, what's going on?" a woman asked from upstairs.

"Well, well, well, look what we have here." Taz shot up the stairs as Javier began to scream.

There was a pretty Mexican chick upstairs in a nightgown. Taz put two hollow points in her face and started walking back down the steps when he heard "Daddy", which froze him mid-step.

"No!" Javier yelled.

Taz went back upstairs, looking in rooms until he got to a little girl's room. There was a little girl in the bed and she was about six years old. She couldn't see him because of how dark it was.

BOOM! BOOM! BOOM! Taz let his pistol bark and went back down the steps to a yelling Javier. Taz hit him in the back of the head with the Glock, knocking him out. Taz then picked him up and carried him down the street to the car.

"You almost got left," Aunt D said.

"Almost just don't count," he shot back.

She drove him to the other side of the city and parked.

"Whose house is this?" Taz asked and Aunt D nodded towards Javier.

"The key is under the welcome mat. I'll be back in the morning."

Taz went and unlocked the door, then carried Javier inside. Taz was walking through the house, checking it out, when he came to a room with a lock on it. He kicked the door open and whistled. It was obviously the room he used to torture people. Taz grabbed Javier up, put him on the table in the room, and strapped him down. Taz did some more searching and found his hockey mask, which he put on, then he saw a camera and tripod facing the table. Taz hit the record button and stepped in front of the camera.

"Hector, this is going to be your fate in the near future," Taz said into the camera.

Taz looked at all the items scattered around the room and grabbed the scissors. He cut all Javier's clothes off, then punched him to wake him up.

"I bet when Hector called you, he didn't tell you that I could get just as nasty as you, if not more," Taz said, circling Javier.

Taz grabbed a surgical scalpel and cut around his wrist, making him holler out.

"Can't nobody hear you," Taz said, peeling the skin off his hand.

Taz stuffed a rag in Javier's mouth because he was tired of hearing him scream. Taz walked to the top of the table and used the scalpel to draw along Javier's hairline and jawbone. Taz peeled the skin off Javier's face the same way he'd probably done his daughters. Javier was moaning and writhing around on the table. Taz paid him no mind. He looked in the corner and saw a defibrillator.

"Oh man! Javier, you're a bad man. You got it all in here. I'm impressed. I bet you never thought your tools would be getting used on your bitch ass, huh?"

Taz left the room to look through the rest of the house. Every other room was normal. He looked in the refrigerator and got a bottle of water. Taz walked back into the room and said to the camera, "The only way this won't happen to you, Hector, is if you go ahead and kill yourself."

Taz took a gulp of water and started back up. He took the rag out of Javier's mouth, grabbed a pair of pliers, and removed Javier's front teeth. Taz had lost himself. All that kept going through his mind was that Javier had cut his babies' faces off and sent them to him

"Fucking pussy-ass wetback!" Taz yelled, getting madder.

He grabbed the machete and chopped the upper part of his foot off.

Javier started going into convulsions and then laid flat.

"Oh no you not, fuck nigga!"

Taz grabbed the defibrillator and charged it up. Taz shocked Javier, trying to bring him back. BOOM! He did it again and checked for a pulse, but didn't feel one. BOOM! Taz shocked him again and got a pulse.

"Yeah, motherfucker! Welcome back!"

Taz tortured Javier until the sun came up. He capped the night off by opening Javier's chest up and sticking the scalpel through his throat.

Taz cleaned up, grabbed the camera, and sat down in the living room to wait for Aunt D. She pulled up two hours later.

"I'm glad to know you're not a complete animal. You still have a heart," she said when he got in the car.

"What're you talking about?"

"Javier's little girl."

"What about the bitch?" Taz questioned.

"You let her live. After I dropped you off, I went by there and got her and took to one of her relatives' houses," she informed him.

Taz had shot three shots into the little girl's headboard to make Javier think he'd killed her. He couldn't bring himself to kill her at that moment. When he saw her, he saw his little girls. Any other time he wouldn't have hesitated.

Aunt D took him to the airport so he could catch his flight back to the States.

"Make sure you give this to Hector for me." Taz gave her the camera that had him torturing Javier.

Taz got on the plane and went to sleep, trying to catch up on the rest he'd missed while torturing Javier.

Nicholas Lock

Chapter 23

Taz was bouncing back and forth from Keishana's to Nesha's to his house with Bella. Junior's first birthday had just passed and Taz was out chilling with Keishana at Hooters.

"I can't believe you got me in here," Keishana said.

"Ain't nothing wrong with Hooters," Taz said as one of the waitresses walked by in her Hooters booty shorts.

"Whatever. So what's been going on with you?"

"Shit, really trying to adjust to life without my girls."

"I feel that, but you know Kiki about to have twins. And she told me she was going to name them Damiyana and D'angelo," Keishana informed him.

Taz already knew Kiki was having twins, a boy and a girl, but they hadn't discussed any names. Even though he'd killed Javier, he still felt empty. Then he'd had to tell D'Azia's and Neveah's mothers what had happened. That had created a whole different kind of ordeal. The shit was stressing him out. This was Keishana's idea to come out because all he was doing was laying around. Taz knew he was going to have to eventually tell Bella about Nesha and his son, but he just wasn't ready to fight. She'd asked him the other day who'd gotten Kiki pregnant and Taz had shrugged his shoulders like he didn't know. Boy, when she found out them was his babies... He didn't even want to think about it.

"Do you want kids, Keishana?"

"What makes you ask that?"

"Just wondering. So do you?"

"What real woman don't want kids? I'm just not willing to take the chance of my baby having the disease."

"I can dig that, and since you not feeling the whole Hooter scene, we can leave. I want to check out Club 305 anyway," Taz said, getting up.

They got in Keishana's dark blue S550 and pulled out. They only had to ride a few minutes down the road before they got to the club. Taz paid for them both and they got a VIP booth. Taz ordered a bottle of Ace of Spades and they chilled out.

"Come on, this is my song!" Keishana grabbed his hand, dragging him to the dance floor "Ayee!" she said, backing her ass up on Taz.

Taz let her dance on him as he grabbed her ass through the Prada jeans she had on. Keishana looked back at Taz and grinned as she threw her ass in a circle. They danced through two songs before they headed back to the booth. Taz popped open the bottle of Ace of Spades and drank straight out of the bottle.

"You so ghetto," she said, taking the bottle from him and turning it up.

"Give my bottle. I don't know where your lips been."

"I know where you want them to be," she said, licking around the rim of the bottle.

"A'ight now." Taz grabbed his dick through his shorts.

They went back and forth taking shots, just enjoying each other's company. This was the first time Taz had so much as smiled since his daughters had disappeared. Taz was feeling himself. He was tipsy as hell and so was Keishana.

"Damn, ma, come dance with me," a tall light-skinned dude came up to Keishana and said.

Taz looked at the dude like he was stupid. He wasn't going to say nothing though. He was going to allow Keishana handle it

"Nah, I'm good, I'm with my peoples." She put her arm around Taz's neck.

"Fuck him! Come fuck with a real nigga," the dude said, grilling Taz.

Taz laughed and leaned back against the booth. He looked the dude up and down and could pretty much tell he wasn't nowhere near his level. Taz was going to try and let him live, but he had better cool it.

"Bitch, fuck you too!"

That was it! Taz grabbed the Ace of Spades bottle and hit him in the head, sending him to the floor. Before Taz could put his foot on him, the bouncers rushed over, breaking it up.

"Let's go." Keishana yanked his arm.

"Who's going to drive?" Taz asked, because they were both borderline drunk. "Fuck it, I got it."

Taz got them to Keishana's house in one piece. They went in and slept the liquor off.

***

The next day, Taz pulled up to his house and saw Kiki's car in his driveway.

"Oh Lord," he thought, getting out of the car.

Taz walked in and Bella and Kiki were in the living room talking with Kiki holding Junior. Taz walked out of the house and came back in to make sure he wasn't tripping.

"What the fuck y'all got going on?" he asked.

"We just talking. Is something wrong with that?" Bella questioned.

Taz pulled his gun out and said, "Yo, y'all better stop playing with me. What type of shit y'all got going on?"

"You not about to shoot us. Put that gun up," Kiki said, bouncing Junior on her knee.

"Da da," Junior said, sliding off Kiki's lap and crawling to him.

"What's up, champ?" Taz started throwing him in the air, making him laugh.

"Stop before you make him sick," said Bella.

"Answer my question. When did you and Kiki become so friendly? The last time I checked, y'all wanted to kill each other." He sat down on the couch.

Bella and Kiki looked at each other and Kiki nodded her head at Bella as if to say it was on her

"Look, Taz, I know you got Kiki pregnant, and I'm cool with it. I've accepted the fact that you love her and that she's a permanent fixture in your life. I even know about the baby you have with the college chick. But I love you so much that I'm willing to overlook all that because I know for a fact you love me. And I'm going to have your last name one day. But I'm telling you right now..." She put her finger in his face "You better not get not one bitch pregnant after this. You got not one, but three bad baby mamas. You want some pussy, it's us or nothing," Bella told him.

"And what you got to say?" Taz asked Kiki.

"Nothing. She said enough," Kiki said nonchalantly.

Something wasn't right! Somebody was rocking somebody to sleep and he couldn't tell who it was, Bella or Kiki. Taz felt like it was Bella because she was the sneaky one of the two. Taz wouldn't put it past Kiki either, but she knew he wasn't playing about something happening to Bella.

"Oh yeah, my mama want to talk to you, and so do Slick," Kiki told him.

Slick? Taz hadn't heard from Slick since the day he'd showed up when the head of the Zoe Pound came to Fayetteville wanting smoke.

"What did he want?"

"He just said he needed to holler at you."

"A'ight. I need to go back to the city anyway. I'll go by there first then on the way back I'll stop and talk to your moms."

Taz booked the next flight out while Bella and Kiki sat in the living room talking. Them talking was going to take some getting used to. He was going to keep his eye on them. You didn't keep two female pit bulls together because they were bound to fight. It was only a matter of time before they clashed and bumped heads. Taz just hoped he was around when it happened.

Taz laid around playing with Junior while he listened to Bella and Kiki talk girl talk.

"Which one of y'all taking me to the airport?"

"I got you. You ready?" Kiki said.

Taz grabbed his bag, kissed Bella and Junior and left out

"What you got up your sleeve?" Taz asked Kiki when they pulled out.

"Who, me?"

"Kiki, don't make me fuck your black ass up," he warned.

"Boy, boo, ain't nobody got nothing up their sleeve. We just decided to kill the little beef we had because once her daddy is dead, all this is going to be over. So I might as well get used to the bean eater."

Taz shook his head. "Behave yourself. I'll be back next week." He kissed Kiki and walked into Miami International Airport.

***

"What's good, bro?" Taz asked Slick.

They were sitting on the west side of Fayetteville in Slick's old school Chevy.

"Shit fucked up! When TK and them got killed, the city took a hit. I ain't been able to get me no real good work or no good prices since."

Since TK, PJ, and Reggie had died, Taz had really fallen back from the work. They were still getting work from Vinnie, but Kiki let her mom distribute it to all the OTF spots. It would be nothing for Taz to put Slick on. He just had to figure out if it was worth the risk. But then again, it wouldn't be a risk. Besides, this was his mans, and Slick had come through in the clutch when he needed him.

"So basically you need some work."

"Pretty much."

"Look, my nigga, I got you. You're a grown man so it ain't nothing I can really tell you, but all I'm going to say is don't make a career out of it."

"Got you, bro." They dapped each other up and sealed the deal.

Taz went straight from Slick's old school to another plane. When he touched down in Atlanta he was bone tired. Kiana picked him up in her yellow Porsche 911.

"I got VIP treatment, didn't I? You probably ain't never picked nobody up from the airport instead of sending someone else to do it," Taz teased.

"I was going to send Meosha, but Kiki called and told me that I better be the one to pick you up," she informed him. "Now that you got my baby pregnant, I can't give you none of this good pussy."

"Who said?" Taz wanted another shot of her cat.

Kiana just looked at him like he should already know.

"What you wanted to talk to me about?"

"Damn, you can't wait until we get to the house?"

Taz sat back and enjoyed the ride. Every time he came to her house, it reminded him of how he wanted to live. When they pulled around to the back, Meosha was riding up on a horse in full riding gear. Taz had always wondered what kind of horses they had in the barn and now he knew. Meosha was sitting on the back of a Clydesdale, the prettiest horse known to man. What made them so pretty to Taz was that not only did they have the hair on the back of their neck, they also had it around their feet.

"You looking like you want to ride or something?" Meosha questioned.

"Maybe tomorrow," Taz said, walking into the house. "Now what's up, Kiana?"

"I need your advice on an issue I have. I'm about to retire from the game and I need someone to take over OTF," Kiana said, looking him in the eye.

"And who do you have in mind?" Taz was hoping like hell she wasn't about to say him because he was going to hurt her feelings.

"At first I thought about Meosha, but she's not street smart. So I need you to convince Kiki to take over."

Nicholas Lock

Chapter 24

Hell no! Kiana must be high. Kiki was about to have his babies, and there was no way he was going to even attempt to try and talk to Kiki about it. That would be going backwards and he didn't believe in that.

"Kiana, you know Kiki pregnant with twins. So you not about to have me to tell her to do nothing that's going to put her or my babies in danger. Being the head of OTF automatically puts a target on her head."

"I had kids and I've been running OTF for years. Besides, she'll have you helping her," Kiana said.

"That's where you're wrong. If she was to decide to take your spot, I'd get my babies from her and go about my business. I ain't got time for this dumb shit my whole life. Shit, ain't you trying to retire right now? So obviously you know what I mean," Taz corrected her.

"Only because I've been doing this for two decades and some. How about you sleep on it and we'll talk in the morning?" Kiana said, walking towards her bedroom.

"Where my room at?" he asked because there were so many bedrooms in the house.

"Use Kiki's. It's at the far end of the house," Kiana said, disappearing into her room.

Taz found Kiki's room and closed the door. Taz kicked his shoes off and stripped down to his boxers. He was so tired that he was asleep the minute his head hit the pillow. Taz woke up in the middle of the night with a pair of soft lips wrapped around his dick.

"I knew you wasn't going to be able to resist getting on this dick," Taz said, running his hand through her hair.

Kiki needed to take some lessons from her mama because it felt like he was in some pussy. She would rotate her head around every time she went down on his dick. She'd take him to the back of her throat and hold him there, then come up to the head of his dick with a pop. She was blowing his mind! Taz grabbed a handful of her hair and began to pump in and out of her mouth. Taz didn't know how she was doing it, but her mouth was so wet that every time he pumped in and out it, was making the same noises a wet pussy made. Taz released inside her mouth, catching her off guard, but she didn't miss a drop. Taz lay back trying to recuperate when she straddled his lap, lowering herself down on his dick.

"Cut the light on so I can see you take this dick," Taz said, but she kept rocking her hips.

"Mmmm," she moaned as Taz reached up and pinched her nipples.

Taz grabbed her hips and started forcing her down so she had to take his whole dick

"Ah! Ah! Ah!" she moaned out.

"You better be quiet before Meosha hears you. Better yet…" Taz leaned up grabbed her and flipped her over so that he was on top. She wrapped her legs around him as he long stroked her

"Mmm! Mmm! Mmm! Mmm!" she continued to moan loudly.

"You must want Meosha to hear you."

Taz pulled out and flipped her onto her stomach. "Toot this butt up."

She tooted her big ass up while laying on her stomach. Taz pushed her ass up and slid back in. Something about the position was too much for her because she started trying to run.

"Oh nah. You about to take all this dick," Taz said, trying to dig her all the way out.

Taz was pounding her out so bad that she had gone from on her stomach to up on one of her knees every stroke she would lift up, trying to keep Taz from going so hard.

"Where you trying to go?" Taz laughed.

Taz got up on his knee so he could have more leverage in his strokes.

"Mmm!" she moaned into a pillow.

Taz started using short, hard strokes, which made her reach one of her hands back. Taz pinned her hand to her back with one hand and used the other one to stick one of his fingers in her butt. Taz kept her in this position until he nutted. He collapsed on the bed and she got up.

"Now you've fucked the mama and both daughters, but your secret is safe with me." She cut the light on.

Taz looked up and saw Meosha standing in his doorway ass naked Oh man, he'd been fucking Meosha the whole time! If Kiki found out, Kiana would most likely be burying another one of her kids. She wouldn't give two fucks if Meosha was her twin. It would be in Meosha's best interest to keep her mouth closed.

**

Taz woke up the next day feeling damn good! They had a big-ass in-ground swimming pool in the backyard and Taz was about to go for a swim. Taz went downstairs and knocked on Kiana's bedroom door.

"Come in."

Taz walked in and Kiana was laying under the covers watching the news.

'Your husband ain't got no swim trunks still here?"

"Look in the closet in one of them drawers."

Taz looked in the drawers, but didn't see any swim trunks.
"Watch out, boy." Kiana pushed Taz to the side.

Taz moved out of the way and then saw she didn't have any clothes on. Taz started to comment, but held his tongue.

"All you had to do was look," Kiana said, holding up a pair of brand new Gucci trunks with the tag still on them.

Kiana went and got back in the bed while Taz went to go put the swim trunks on so he could get in the pool. As he was going back to Kiki's room to change, he saw Meosha asleep in her room. Taz crept in her room, closing the door behind him. He walked up to her bed and snatched the comforter back.

"What the fuck was you thinking about?" Taz asked, looking at her near-perfect body.

"I was thinking I wanted some dick," Meosha said, sliding her hand between her legs.

"Yo, check this shit out. I don't know what type of shit you on, but you going to have to dead it. You cool peoples and I want to see you live a long life. Fucking with me is going to get you killed. Kiki not going to care about you being her sister," Taz tried warning her.

"Ain't nobody scared of Kiki! I'll fuck her up too!"

Taz just looked at her because he had seen what happened the last time Kiki got mad at Meosha. Kiki had dropped her with one punch.

"Just let the shit go, Meosha," Taz said and then walked out.

Taz went and put the swim trunks on and then went to the pool. Taz got in and started swimming laps. He swam until he got tired, then he turned onto his back and floated.

Taz was floating around the pool relaxing when Kiana walked up and asked, "Have you thought about what I asked you?"

"Honestly, no. Your daughter is grown and she's going to do what she want to do regardless of what you say."

"I noticed you said regardless of what I say, but what about what you say?" She sat down at the edge of the pool, letting her legs dangle in the water.

"You know whatever I say she's going to do for the most part, but don't worry. I'm not going to tell her not to. I'm going to let her make her own decision. But like I said before, if she do, I'm taking my babies," Taz reminded her.

"Think about how much money y'all could make if y'all run OTF. You and Kiki would be unstoppable."

"If you haven't noticed, my money long now. And it's legal money at that. I ain't got to worry about the police or the jackboys running in my shit," Taz bragged. "Enough of that. I'm trying to learn how to ride one of them horses."

"Get dressed and I'll teach you," Kiana said, going into the house.

Taz went in and got dressed. He put on some shorts and a wife beater and sat down in the kitchen to wait for Kiana. She came out in a yellow sundress and some flats.

"You're going to ride with that on?"

"I'm not riding. You is."

Taz followed her out to the horse barn. Taz saw the one he wanted to ride as soon as he stepped in. It was all-black horse with white feet.

"No, no," Kiana said when he walked up to the stall.

"What's up?"

"She's mean as hell. That's Boots. She don't really let people ride her or really even touch her, for that matter," Kiana told him.

Taz stood at Boots's stall, looking at her look at him.

"We're going to get along just fine, ain't we, Boots?" Taz fed her a sugar cube. Taz tried to rub her neck and she snorted, shaking her head from side to side.

"She bites," Kiana said, watching from afar.

"She's not going to let you ride her. She won't let no one ride her." Meosha appeared out of nowhere.

"I ain't never met a female that didn't fuck with me, whether it be sexually or just as friends. Ain't that right, Boots?" Taz fed her another sugar cube and rubbed her neck.

Seeing that she let him touch her, he felt comfortable enough to open the stall door. He stepped in, grabbed a brush, and started brushing her coat.

"I'll be damned," Kiana said in disbelief.

"Show me how to put the reins and the saddle on," Taz said.

Kiana showed Taz what to do and how to do it. "Now look, Taz, be careful with her. I don't need nothing happening to her," Kiana warned him. "She cost me more than the average person's house and car put together."

"Yeah, right."

"Taz, that horse cost me seven figures - seven and a half, to be exact," Kiana stated. "That's the going rate for a Clydesdale. Look it up," she said, seeing the look on his face.

He shook his head and hopped up on the horse. Taz took hold off the reins and Boots trotted off. It was weird at first, but Taz got the hang of it immediately.

"You're a natural," Kiana told him.

Taz could feel the power of the horse under him. He kicked his feet and Boots shot off. She broke into a full gallop into the woods behind Kiana's house. Taz let Boots run. He just enjoyed the run. She had to have run the trail before because she seemed like she knew where she was going. She ran for about ten minutes, then came to a stop by a big lake. Boots leaned down to drink while Taz took in the scenery.

It was a relaxing scene. He let her drink her fill, then put her into a slow trot back to Kiana's house. Kiana showed Taz how to rub her down, then he put her back in her stall and walked back to the house.

"Kiki just called and said you need to call her ASAP," Meosha said, smiling.

I know this bitch ain't did no stupid shit and told Kiki, Taz thought to himself while going to grab his phone.

"Why the fuck you ain't been answering your phone?" Kiki asked when she picked up.

"I was out riding one of the horses. Now what's up?"

"You need to come home now, right now! I think somebody took Bella. The front door was hanging off the hinges and the house was trashed. And there's a puddle of blood in the kitchen," Kiki told him and he hung up.

"Kiana, if you had something to do with, this I'm going to kill you," he said, grabbing the keys to Meosha's Challenger and running out of the house, leaving Kiana with a confused look on her face.

Nicholas Lock

Chapter 25

Taz called Bella's phone back to back trying to get in contact with her. He called her the whole ride to Miami. His mind was all over the place. There had to be a reasonable explanation for this. Taz tried to convince himself everything was okay, even though he knew the odds weren't good. He went down the list of people he had problems with and all he could come up with was the Mexican Cartel. Taz knew Hector wouldn't hurt Bella, but the more he thought about it, the more that scenario didn't make sense. The cartel soldiers listened to Bella too. The blood was throwing Taz for a loop.

Then there was Kiana. He knew Hector had her husband and sons killed. And no matter how cool she acted, she wanted revenge, and what better way to get revenge than to kill Hector's last living child? But where the fuck was Junior at? Nothing made sense! Taz had already eliminated Kiki because even if she would've done something to Bella, which she knew better, she wouldn't do anything to his son. Taz was getting a headache trying to rack his brain to figure out what was going on.

He pulled up to his house and ran in. His house was a complete mess. There was furniture turned over, drawers pulled out, and glass everywhere. It seemed like they were looking for something. Taz saw blood drops from the front door to the kitchen, where there was a puddle of blood.

"I didn't touch anything. I wanted you to see how everything was." Kiki came up behind him, making him jump

"This might not be her blood." Taz bent, down picking up two shell casings. They were .380 shells, Bella's go-to weapon. That eliminated the Mexican Cartel because Bella wouldn't have had to shoot them. They obeyed her like they obeyed Hector. All that was left was OTF.

"Tell your mama she already knows what time it is." Taz looked at Kiki.

"She didn't have anything to do with this. I already talked to her. She would've told me."

"Are you sure about that?" Taz questioned. OTF was the only logical answer. There wasn't anybody else to consider

"Talk to her yourself. Her and my twin are on their way down here right now."

Taz ignored her and started cleaning the house up. Kiki helped him without being asked. They had everything back in order and cleaned up in no time.

"I'm going to go check on Nesha. Call me when your mama get in town," he stated.

Taz tried calling Nesha, but she didn't pick up. She was probably mad that he hadn't called her in a few days. He definitely didn't have time to deal with her attitude or one of her temper tantrums. And that's exactly what he was probably going to have to deal with.

He let himself into her apartment and got a shock. The apartment was empty! She was going too far with this shit now. Taz walked through the whole apartment and it was completely empty. Nesha was going to fuck around and make him choke the shit out of her. He walked out and went on Miami's campus to look for her. Taz walked all through the campus and he couldn't find her. Something told Taz to go by the school office.

"Excuse me, Miss?" Taz approached the secretary.

"Yes."

"I'm looking for my girlfriend, but I can't find her and her apartment is empty like she moved out."

"What's her name?"

"Quanesha Duvalier."

The secretary typed the name into her computer. "It says right here she's no longer enrolled."

"Okay, thank you."

Nesha was going to make Taz kill her. She was all the way out of order for the stunt she was pulling right now. She was blowing this shit out of proportion. Now Taz didn't know where either of his sons was, and it was beginning to grate on his nerves. One thing he did know was that Ares was safe with his mama and he also knew that Bella would die before she let someone harm Junior.

***

"Listen, Taz, you have my word I had nothing to do with Bella's disappearance, nor did I have any knowledge of it. My peoples didn't have anything to do with it either," Kiana told Taz.

They were in Kiki's living room. Taz was leaning up against the fireplace while Kiki tried to plead her case. Every minute that passed, Taz got madder and madder. He'd lost Neveah and D'Azia, and he'd be damned if he was going to lose Junior and Ares too.

"Come sit down." Meosha patted the seat beside her.

"Kiana, I'm going to take your word for it because I feel we got a good enough relationship that you're not going to sit in here and lie to my face. But just in case you have a misunderstanding of where your daughter stands, Kiki, who you rocking with no matter what?" Taz put her on the spot.

Kiki nodded her head in Taz's direction and said, "You, bae."

"So please don't let it come out that you're lying to me."

"You need to relax a little bit while we come up with a plan on how to find out where your kids are. Come let me give you a massage real quick," Meosha continued.

Taz cut his eyes in Kiki's direction because he knew she was bound to say something.

"Meosha, you better quit while you're ahead," Kiki warned.

"Girl, boo, I ain't thinking about no Taz. Stop being so insecure." Meosha waved her off.

"If I wasn't pregnant, I'd beat your ass, but don't try your luck."

"Both of y'all be quiet! It's more important matters going on than y'all's bickering," Kiana scolded them.

Somebody rang Kiki's doorbell. Kiki went to get the door while Taz tried to come up with an idea on how to find Bella and Nesha.

"Taz, are you okay?" Keishana asked, walking into the house and hugging Taz.

"I'm good. You?"

"You know me, same old thing, just working and relaxing," Keishana said, sitting down beside Taz.

"Oh shit!" Taz said as his phone rang, showing he had a text from Bella. "Here go Bella right here." Taz opened the text and dropped the phone.

"What is it?" Kiki asked.

Keishana picked the phone up, looked at the text, and covered her mouth. It was a picture text and it showed Bella tied up and bloody. There was no sign of Junior in the picture.

"Aw man," Kiki and Kiana said when they saw the picture.

"They just sent a text," Kiki said.

Taz grabbed the phone and read the text. It said "an eye for an eye". *Who the fuck is playing these type of games?* Taz asked himself. They had his baby tied up and bleeding and he still didn't know where Junior was. That was irking him more than anything. Why send a picture of Bella and not Junior? Taz couldn't take losing another child, especially his firstborn son.

"Kiki, let me holler at you," Keishana said.

Kiki and Keishana went in the kitchen and Taz walked out. He needed to be alone. Being alone would help him think better. Taz walked next door to his house and laid down in the bed. Taz could smell Bella in the sheets. He missed his bitch. An eye for an eye? Taz had done so much dirt in his life that he had absolutely no idea who had Bella. He was getting a headache from trying to figure things out, plus he hadn't eaten anything all day.

"Taz, where you at?" Kiki yelled.

"The bedroom."

Kiki, Keishana, Kiana, and Meosha busted in his room, cutting the light on.

"What was Quadree's last name?" Kiki asked.

"I don't remember. Why, what's up?" Taz asked, confused. He'd killed Quadree years ago and gone to prison for it.

"I need to see something. Where your motion discovery at?"

"The closet," Taz said, getting up.

Kiki grabbed his motion and turned to the page that had Quadree's name on it. "Now what's Nesha's last name?"

"Duvalier." Taz was trying to figure out where she was going with this.

"And guess what Quadree's rat-ass last name was? Duvalier," Kiki said.

"So what, Kiki? That's probably a common name for the islands." Taz tried defending Nesha.

"Keishana, tell him." Kiki put her hand on her hip.

"Taz, you remember when I told you she looked familiar? Well, the reason she looked familiar was because I seen her at Zion's house. When you sent me down here to get at him, I was at his house and she came over. They went in another room and talked for about fifteen minutes then she left," Keishana informed him.

"Keishana, why the fuck you just now telling me this shit?"

"I told you I couldn't remember where I'd seen her, and then you told me how she used to go to Fayetteville State, so I figured that's where I had seen her at."

Taz sat down on his bed and put his head in his hands. There had to be a reasonable explanation for her knowing Zion. Who knows? They might've been fucking. Shit just didn't make sense. There was no way Nesha was connected to the Zoe Pound. Not prissy-ass Nesha. Taz had to make her take his gun that day.

"Answer my phone, Kiki," Taz said.

"It's Nesha." She handed him the phone

Taz put it on speaker phone and asked, "Nesha, where the fuck you at?"

"Heyyy, baby daddy! You miss me?"

"I'm not really in the mood to play. Where my son?"

"Well be like that then, fuck boi! But da jokes on ya. Mi see ya still ain't figured it out."

"What is you talking about?" Taz asked, even though he already knew.

"Mi name is Quanesha Duvalier! Ya know da nigga ya kilt named Quadree? Dat was mi brudda, pussy boi! But mi have both ya sons and ya wifey. Ya taught ya just kill mi brudda an noting happen?"

"Ha, ha, ha, Nesha, you must be out of your mind. The same thing that happened to your rat-ass brudda can happen to you. And just so you know, I'm not the one who killed your bitch-ass brudda," Taz mocked her.

"It not matta now. How it feel to have something ya love taken from ya? Huh? Now ya neva see eitha of ya sons again!" Nesha said confidently.

"Don't be so sure about that. Nesha, I'll make a deal with you. Give me Bella and both my sons and you have my word I won't kill you." Taz tried giving her a way out.

"Nice try, fuck boi! If mi was in da States mi might would worry, but mi in Haiti where ya can't do nuttin ta mi. Ha! Ha! Oh, ya taught mi was from Barbados? Got ya again," Nesha rubbed it in.

"I tried to save you. It's your funeral. But let me ask you a question, little girl. Why did you let me get you pregnant?"

Nesha got quiet for a minute then said in a low voice, "Dat wasn't supposed ta happen."

Taz hung the phone up. He didn't want to hear anymore. He'd been played like a fiddle and that shit was eating him up. Taz thought he was done with the whole Quadree and Zoe Pound situation. He'd killed the head of the Zoe Pound a while ago and they were still fucking his life up from the grave. Nesha had played the long game to the fullest. Taz thought he'd been playing chess, but Nesha had just taken his queen and had him in check!

"What's the plan, bae?" Kiki asked

"I'm going to Haiti to get my babies and Bella and kill Nesha."

Nicholas Lock

Chapter 26

"Haiti isn't as little as you may think. You need to find out what city she in and I think I can help with that," Kiana said.

Taz heard her, but he didn't respond. He was focused on how he was going to pull this stunt off. He was in the blind because he wasn't going to have a gun when he first got over there, so he was going to have to try and buy one off the street. Then to top it off, Haiti was full of Zoe Pound niggas, so Taz had to be on his shit.

"I'm going with you," Kiki said.

Taz looked at her swollen stomach then at her face and went back to trying to formulate a plan. He didn't have to tell Kiki that she was dead. His look said it all.

"Nigga, this stomach don't mean I can't shoot! I still shoot better than most niggas! You're not going by yourself!" Kiki yelled at Taz.

Taz didn't respond. He hadn't said two words since getting the phone call from Nesha.

Taz was still trying to figure out how he missed the signs, because there were always signs of deceit. He just had to recognize them. The more he thought about it, the more he had to applaud her mental. This was years in the making. She'd played the ultimate long game. But then again, could there have been someone else behind the scenes giving her directions? Because when he asked her why she let him get her pregnant, she said it wasn't supposed to happen.

"What number did she call from?" asked Kiana.

Kiana got the number and told someone on her phone, then a couple minutes later, she wrote something down on a piece of paper and hung up.

"I got it. She's in Port-au-Prince. I had my homegirl at the police department triangulate the phone's location." Kiana narrowed the search down for Taz.

"Kiana, it's over two million people in Port-au-Prince, but that helped. At least I don't got to go searching all over Haiti."

"I'll go with you," Meosha volunteered.

"Bitch, please! What you going to do, look pretty?" Kiki asked.

"Nah, Meosha, you'd be easy to spot. You and Kiki is twins, remember?" Taz told her.

"So you're going to go at this by yourself?" Kiana asked. "That's just not smart."

"It's really my only option. Taking Kiki or Meosha is out of the question and Keishana don't live that life."

"I can go then because you're going to need some kind of assistance and I'm the most qualified."

"Ma, hell no!" her daughters said in unison.

Taz was going to object, but then again, Kiana had built OTF up from the ground up. He knew she could be ruthless if need be. "You think you still got it? You know you getting kind of long in the tooth," Taz joked. Kiana was in her late forties.

"I probably got more than you! I was doing this when you was a snotty-nosed little boy."

"Have your shit ready. We're going to book a flight for Friday morning," Taz said.

"Book a flight? No, honey, have you forgot what I do for a living? I run the biggest investigation firm in the U.S. If only you knew! I have dirt on a lot of billionaires. I can borrow one of their jets. That way we won't have to worry about how we're going to get guns. We can take them with us."

"Bet. Go ahead and set that up. Kiki, you come here." Taz walked in the bathroom and closed the door. "Look, you need to calm your ass down! Have you forgot that you have my babies in your stomach? You fuck around and lose my babies because you being extra, and I'm going to fuck you up," he warned.

"You not going to do shit!" Kiki grabbed him by his neck and stuck her tongue in his mouth. She stuck her tongue in his ear and put her hand down his shorts, causing him to get hard, but he pushed her away.

"Nah, I'm good," Taz told her and then walked out, leaving Kiki thirty-eight hot.

***

Taz and Kiana boarded a private jet owned by one of her clients.

"This shit exclusive!" Taz said, boarding the plane. The inside looked like a penthouse in New York or South Beach Miami. There was a bedroom with a king-sized bed and everything. This was big dog status.

A flight attendant that looked just like Kendall Jenner came up and said, "Let me know if there's anything you need."

"You come with the plane?" Taz asked.

"Yes sir."

"Leave that woman alone," Kiana said, grabbing a seat.

"So I can use anything on the plane?" Taz continued.

"Yes sir."

"Does that include you?" Taz asked, and Kiana shook her head.

"I'm not sure what you mean," she said, but Taz could see the slut in her. He was almost a hundred percent sure she knew exactly what he meant.

"Do you know first aid?"

"Yes sir, I'm required to know."

"Well, I have some swelling that won't go down. Let's go in the back. I don't want to disturb Ms. Kiana."

She led Taz to the bedroom and he locked the door behind them.

"Where's the swelling, sir?" she asked. Taz took his shorts and boxers off, revealing a swollen dick. Her eyes got big as a crackhead's after their morning hit.

"It won't go down," Taz said, stroking his dick.

"Um, sir, I don't know how I can help you," were the words she said, but she made no effort to leave.

"I can show you. All you have to do is hike your skirt up and lean over the bed."

"I don't know about that. I could lose my job," she said, leaning over the bed, pulling her skirt up, and spreading her legs.

Taz walked up behind her, pulled her G-string to the side, and slid into his dick's favorite place. She immediately started trying to run from him. Taz was just trying to get a quick nut so he undid her ponytail and wrapped her hair around his hand a few times.

"Uh! Uh! Uh! Uh!" she hollered as Taz hit her with short fast strokes "I'm cumming!" she yelled.

"Get on your knees. Hurry up!" Taz stroked his dick a few times, sending streams of nut all over her face. Just as Taz thought, she was a slut! She started wiping her face with her hands and licking her fingers clean.

"If there's any other way I can help, don't hesitate to ask," she said, fixing her clothes and walking out.

Taz walked out and grabbed a seat beside Kiana. She cut her eyes at him and shook her head. Taz reclined his seat and enjoyed the rest of his flight because when he touched down, it was going to be all gas, no brakes.

They touched down at the airport and were able to get their luggage right through without being checked. *The perks of the rich*, Taz thought to himself. They looked like everyday tourists. Kiana was wearing a pink floral sundress and some white open toe pumps while Taz had on some blue Bermuda shorts, a white T-shirt, and some white Gucci boating shoes. There was a car waiting for them outside to take them to their hotel downtown.

"Go ahead and change. I'm about to go in here and get strapped up, then I'm going out to find my babies. Time is of the essence."

"All I need is five minutes," Kiana said, getting out of the car.

When Taz walked in his room, he stripped down and put on some camouflage cargo shorts, a green T-shirt, and some camouflage sevens. Taz put his dreads up in a bun because him walking with long dreads with white tips would attract attention, and that's the last thing he needed. He put extra clips into the pockets of his shorts, made sure his vest was good, then headed next door to Kiana's room.

"You said all you needed was five minutes," Taz said when she let him in and he saw all she had on were some boy shorts and a bra.

"If you really want to know, I called my homegirl to see if she could narrow the location of the phone down. You can thank me later. And where is you going, to the club?" she asked, looking at his outfit.

"Get dressed." He sat down on her bed

Kiana put her vest on, then she donned some khaki capris, a cream-colored shirt, and some khaki-colored Nike running shoes. They walked out of the hotel and Kiana walked up to a black Hummer.

"Drive," She tossed him some keys.

"Where you get this?"

"Less talking, more driving," Kiana stated, climbing inside the Hummer. "We need to go to the outskirts of the city. She said that the phone pinged off a phone tower in that area."

Taz drove through the city taking it in. Parts of the city was okay, but other parts were run down. The farther they got from the city, the more rundown things became. They were now in the slums. Kiana put one in the head of each of her .45's and looked out the window. They were still going to be in the blind because they didn't have an exact location. As Taz drove, all he saw were rugged-looking niggas with rude dreads. This was going to be crazy.

"Pull over right there." Kiana pointed.

Taz pulled over and she started rolling her window down.

"What you doing?"

"I got this," she said, calling an old man over to the truck. "I'm looking for my homegirl. Do you know her?" She showed him a picture of Nesha.

"She stay about a mile down the road. Drive straight until you have to make a left or a right, turn right, then make the first left. She stays in a white house. You can't miss it."

"Thank you." Kiana gave him a fifty dollar bill.

"That wasn't smart. What if that would've been one of her peoples?"

"I would've put two in his face," she said nonchalantly.

While following the directions from the old man, the sun started to set. Taz pulled onto her street and saw why the dude said you couldn't miss it. It was easily the biggest house on the block and also the newest, like it had recently been built.

"Look, they don't know you, so go ahead and knock since you're into taking risks." He looked her way.

"I'm all the way like that," Kiana said, getting out and walking up to the door.

A middle-aged woman answered the door and Kiana knocked her out with the butt of her gun.

"Oh my God. What is this woman doing?" Taz said, rushing up to the house. "What you doing?" Taz asked, and she put her finger to her lips.

Kiana gave directions with her hands, telling Taz to go upstairs and she was going down. Taz crept up the stairs, trying not to make any noise. He heard voices coming from a room to his left. He kicked the door in and saw Nesha, his son Ares, and another chick. Nesha's eyes got big as hell when she saw Taz.

"Who are you?" the chick asked.

Taz shot her in the face and told Nesha, "Bitch, I should kill you right now. Now where my son and Bella at?"

"You good, Taz?" Kiana asked up the stairs.

"Yeah, come here," he said. "Nesha, you got two seconds to tell me where they at or I'm going to kill you here and now."

"Lookie here," Kiana said upon seeing Nesha.

Taz grabbed his son Ares up and looked at Nesha before walking out of the room, leaving her with Kiana. Taz sat Ares down on the couch just as a shot went off upstairs and Nesha screamed. Taz grabbed the lady up and dragged her away from the door into the kitchen, where he tied her hands behind her back. Taz heard two more shots and knew it was over for Nesha.

"Come on! Come on!" Kiana said.

Taz followed her outside to a shed with a lock on it. Kiana shot it off and they pulled the door open. There lay Bella, bruised and bloody. He rushed over to her.

"Baby, wake up! Bella!" he yelled, and she opened her eyes. When she saw Taz, she latched her arms around his neck and started sobbing.

"I'm sorry! I'm so sorry! I tried, but there wasn't anything I could do!"

"You good, bae, I got you now." He picked her up.

"No! It's not good! They killed Junior!" she yelled and he almost dropped her.

"Say what?" Taz hoped his ears had deceived him.

"They killed our baby!" she cried in his neck.

He carried her into the house and sat her down. "Now you said they killed Junior. Who is they?" Taz thought Bella might've been tripping

"Nesha and him." She pointed as a heavyset dude came through the door with long dreads.

Chapter 27

BAH! BAH! BAH! BAH!

Kiana started firing her .45's in the dude's direction, making him dive back out the door. Taz took off after him, but he ran between some houses and disappeared.

"Come on!" Taz yelled to them, because he was sure the dude was going to get some backup.

Kiana came out of the house helping a limping Bella, who was carrying Ares. They got in the Hummer and Taz mashed the gas. He wasn't planning on being there when reinforcements showed up.

"They're fueling the plane up right now," Kiana said, getting off the phone. All they had to do was make it to the airport.

Taz, looking in the back, saw Bella clutching a scared Ares to her chest. Four muscle cars and a truck passed him going the other way.

"That dude was in the first car," Kiana said.

"They're turning around," Bella said from the backseat.

Kiana rolled her window down and when they got close, she leaned out the window and started shooting her .45's. Ares started crying from all the noise and chaos going on around him.

"Hand me that case on the backseat," Kiana told Bella.

She got the case and opened it. There was a carbon 15 inside. She put it together and slapped a banana clip in.

KAH! KAH! KAH! KAH! KAH!

Kiana unloaded a barrage of bullets on the cars, keeping them from getting too close. She emptied that clip and reached in the car and grabbed another one. Kiana was cutting up! Kiki wasn't fucking with her mama. They were almost to the airport when one of the cars rammed them from behind and another car pulled up alongside of them and started shooting. Taz jerked the Hummer to the left and slammed into the car, sending it off the road. Taz turned into the airport parking lot. The first car pulled in behind them, but the other ones stopped. Taz pulled to the front and stopped. He grabbed the carbon 15 from Kiana and hopped out. He was about to spray, but some of Haiti's finest pulled in. Taz and the dude mugged each other as he pulled back out of the parking lot. Taz grabbed Ares from Bella and he instantly quieted down.

"You miss Daddy, little man?"

"Come on," Kiana said, leading the way.

Taz helped Bella into the airport and onto the jet. Taz got the first aid kit and started doctoring her up. Her injuries weren't bad. They were mostly superficial.

"Now what happened, Bella?" Taz asked, trying to put Ares to sleep.

"I was at the house cleaning up when the doorbell rang. I went to the door and it was your baby mama, so I let her in. As soon as I did that, she started attacking me, then that heavyset dude and four other men came in. Junior was in his car seat in the kitchen so I ran in there to grab Junior. My gun was on the counter. I was able to shoot one of them, but somebody grabbed me from behind. Next thing I know I was in that shack and Nesha would come out and beat on me every day." She started to cry.

"You good now, baby." Taz gave a sleeping Ares to Kiana so he could comfort Bella.

"I'm not good! I couldn't protect our baby! Did you not see the grave? They killed our son and buried him in the backyard like he was a dog or something." Bella cried into Taz's chest.

Taz had seen the little grave, but he thought it was probably a pet, not his fucking son. Things were starting to be a little
too much! He'd lost his two daughters and now a son - his
firstborn son, at that. He was at his wit's end. There was no
way Taz could afford to go toe to toe with the Mexican Cartel
and the Zoe Pound Mafia at the same time. The last time he'd
gone at it with the Zoe Pound, he'd won by killing the head
nigga Zion and his son Gutta, but they'd been able to kill his
little sister in the process. Taz knew for certain he wasn't going to lose another child.

"Give me my baby," Bella said, confusing Taz. "Give me
Ares. She took my baby, so now Ares is mine." Bella clutched
Ares to her chest.

Taz didn't know what to say. He looked to Kiana and she
shook her head as if to say leave her be.

"Come on, Bella." Taz led her to the bedroom. "Get some
rest." He closed the door.

"Let her have her way," Kiana said when Taz sat down
beside her. "That's one of the most traumatic things a woman
can face is the loss of a child. It was her first and only child,
plus it was a boy, which makes it all worse. She's going to
substitute Ares for Junior. What is Ares, about three months?"
Kiana asked and Taz nodded a yes. "He'll grow up knowing
her as his mother and she'll treat him as such." She dropped
some jewels on him.

Taz was going to take her advice and let Bella raise Ares
as her own. It couldn't hurt anything since his real mom was
dead.

"Is there anything you need, sir?" the flight attendant
asked, licking her lips.

"No, I'm straight." Taz wasn't in the mood. His mind was
having a battle. He wanted to leave the issue where it was, but

the gangsta in Taz was telling him dude had to die for killing his son. There was just no way around it.

"Let me get home and check to see who he is and then we can proceed from there," Kiana said as if reading his mind.

With that said, Taz reclined his seat and slept the rest of the flight.

***

After being home for a week, Taz still couldn't get the heavyset dude off his mind. He'd made his mind up to bust dude's brain. He was just waiting on Kiana to give him the rundown.

Bella had settled back into things. She was good now, but she still had her moments. When Taz first brought her home, she would have nightmares every night. Now it was only every now and then. She took being Ares's mother seriously! It was hard for Taz to get any time with him. Bella wouldn't let Ares out of her sight and if it wasn't Taz, you couldn't even hold him. Taz had been fucking her almost every night trying to get her pregnant. Then Kiki was at the house so much Taz told her to get a room. Kiki and Bella had become the best of friends. They had taken to staying up late talking into the night. Taz was going to try and get a threesome if they kept it up.

"Let me see him." Taz grabbed Ares from Bella. "You not about to be babying him up. I'm not about to have no soft-ass son."

"Boy, boo," she said, curling her feet under her.

Taz had been making it his mission to spend as much time as possible with Ares. Taz knew he could leave this earth at any moment, so he had to cherish every moment. Taz couldn't wait for Kiki to drop his twins so he could spoil them, especially his daughter.

"Baby, what does Ares mean?" Bella asked.

"Ares was the Greek God of war. I'm going to Atlanta later on. Are you coming?"

"Of course. Let me go grab some things."

While Bella went to get her stuff together, Taz called Kiki.

"We leaving to go to Atlanta in a little bit. You riding with us?"

"Yeah, I'll be over there in a minute," she said and then hung up.

Taz carried Ares upstairs to his room and laid him in his playpen while he packed his diaper bag. Taz was going up to Atlanta to see what Kiana had found out and also to get Bella out of the house for a little bit. She had been cooped up in the house a little too much. It was probably going to be good for her to be around some women.

"Dang, bae, come on!" Bella yelled from downstairs.

"How you going to rush me when it was my idea?" he yelled back, making Ares laugh. "What you laughing at, man? Huh? You laughing at your daddy, boy?" Taz asked, making him smile, showing off his gums.

"What are you doing up here?" Bella asked, walking into the room with Kiki behind her, looking sexy as hell.

Kiki was already thick, but the babies were putting more weight on her. Her thighs, ass, and breasts had gotten bigger, and she had that glow. He was fucking her tonight.

"I'm glad y'all came up here. Here, take this." Taz gave Ares to Bella and gave Kiki the diaper bag and went to the garage.

Kiki and Bella came and got in the G-wagon five minutes later. Taz had made a mistake in inviting Kiki along. The whole ride to Atlanta he had to listen to Kiki and Bella talk about shopping and clothes. He was so glad to be pulling into Kiana's driveway.

"Oh my God, this is beautiful!" Bella took in Kiana's house.

"Come in, let me show you around," Kiki said. They took off.

"Y'all not going to grab no bags?" Taz yelled after them, but they kept walking.

"It's just me and you, baby boy."

Taz grabbed Ares out of his car seat and walked around to the back of the house. As soon as he bent the corner, Boots came galloping up to him. She started nudging him with her nose. Ares found this amusing because he started laughing and bouncing in his arms.

"She remembers you," Kiana told him, standing on the back porch. "Give me the baby."

Taz gave Ares to Kiana and he walked Boots back to the barn. He gave her some sugar cubes and brushed her coat.

"Bring her over here," Meosha said.

Taz led Boots over to a pool they had inside the barn. Boots got in and started walking. There was a treadmill built into the bottom of the pool so the horses could exercise.

"You giving me some dick tonight," Meosha said.

"Meosha, stop the bullshit before I tell Kiki," he warned.

KAH! KAH! KAH! KAH! KAH!

Taz jumped to the ground as shots started to ring out. Taz looked around and then he realized he wasn't being shot at. He peeked out of the barn and saw what looked like an army of Mexican Cartel members running up to the back of Kiana's house.

"You got a gun?" Taz asked Meosha.

She handed him a 9 and Taz came out of the barn firing. Taz was able to drop two of them before they realized someone was behind him. Some of them turned their guns in his direction. Taz ducked back in the barn as they sent a wave of bullets his way. He needed to get his hands on one of the choppas they were shooting.

TAT! TAT! TAT! TAT! TAT! TAT! Taz looked and saw Kiki in one of the upstairs windows busting an AR15. Taz ran and grabbed one of the AK's and tossed Meosha her 9 back. He had to get to the house where Ares was. He was hoping Bella had Ares because that way he knew he'd be safe. The esse's wouldn't hurt Bella.

Taz and Meosha shot their way inside the house. They killed the rest of the esse's, but the damage had already been done.

"Mama!" Meosha yelled, seeing Kiki cradling a dead Kiana in her lap. Taz saw the fire in Kiki's eyes and he knew it was going to take Jesus coming back to stop Kiki from cutting up. Pregnant or not.

Nicholas Lock

Chapter 28

Kiana had a lot of love in Atlanta. There were so many flowers and balloons at her house. They had just laid Kiana to rest and they were all at Kiana's house eating. There were at least a hundred and fifty OTF members scattered throughout the house. Kiki had been solemn ever since her mom had gotten killed. Taz knew it had taken years for them to reconnect but when they did, they had clicked even after the rocky start. Kiki was just like her mom. She had the same bossy attitude and smart mouth. Meosha was also taking it hard because she hadn't said too much of anything. She wasn't even pushing up on Taz anymore.

"Everybody listen up!" Kiki yelled. Kiki was standing on the walkway upstairs that looked down on the living room. She had everybody's attention then she continued by saying, "My mama is gone and she left me in charge of OTF. If anybody has an issue with this, you need to speak up now or forever hold your peace." She looked down at everybody.

Taz was hot! But now wasn't the time to voice his frustration because he didn't want to undermine her authority in front of everyone. He hoped nobody fell for her trick and said anything, but there was always one.

"Yeah, I got an issue with it. Why is it you? I know I'm not the only one that's wondering this," a dark-skinned dude asked.

"Anybody else? Kiki asked, and no one else stepped up.

BOOM! Kiki blew the top of his head off

"Don't think for one minute that shit is sweet! It's a reason my mama left me in charge! There are going to be some changes that's going to benefit us all. Starting with us expanding to other cities and states." Kiki took charge.

Taz wasn't going to front Kiki; was a born leader. But he still was going to let her know the whole leading OTF idea was dead. She had better train Meosha to take over.

Taz walked into the kitchen. Kiki had a whole army under her command now, at least until Taz convinced her otherwise. Until then, Taz could guarantee Kiki was going to make the OTF soldiers rain down hell on the Mexican Cartel.

Bella and Kiki were still good, but you could tell things were a little weird. Bella's dad was the reason both of Kiki's parents were dead and Kiki was in the process of trying to kill Bella's dad. They were in a murder triangle.

"What's on your mind?" a Puerto Rican chick asked.

"It don't even matter. You can't help," Taz responded.

"How you know?" She slid up on Taz.

"Vanessa, you might want to ease up. That dick right there will cost you your life," one of Kiki's cousins said. "That's Kiki's dick."

"What Kiki's dick?" asked Kiki, coming into the kitchen. Her cousin pointed at Taz.

Kiki walked up to Taz and kissed him on the lips, but Taz didn't return the kiss. She knew he was mad at her just by his response. Kiki led him into her mama's room and took a seat "What's your issue?" she asked.

"So you're just going to take over OTF without even asking me how I felt about it?"

"This is what my mama wanted. She knew I'd be the one to take this to the next level."

"Why not let Meosha run shit and you run the investigation firm?" Taz questioned.

"And how long do you think OTF would stay afloat with Meosha at the helm?" she shot right back.

"You know what? Do you, Kiki, but when you have my babies, I'm taking them and I'm leaving the States." Taz walked out, leaving her to weigh her options.

***

"The city ain't been the same since you been gone, my nigga," Slick told Taz.

They were sitting in Slick's house in Montebello on the west side of Fayetteville. It had been a while since Taz had been home to chill. Since putting Slick on he'd taken off - all the way off. He was the go-to man in the city. He'd moved out of Lafayette Plantation, which was a big trailer park, to the suburbs. He was living life.

"We hitting the club tonight too! These motherfuckers is going to go crazy when you step inside, especially the hoes," Slick said.

"I don't know, boy, I been trying to lay low."

"Fuck that, we out there!"

"Out where?" Slick's wifey asked, standing with her hand on her hip.

"Nothing," Slick responded quickly.

"Taz, where y'all going?"

"Nah, Erica, don't put me in that. Matter of fact, hit me up, Slick, I'm about to hit the mall real quick." Taz left Slick to deal with his lady.

Taz went to the Cross Creek Mall. It seemed like ages since he'd stepped foot inside of it. Taz's first stop was Lid's. He bought a black and gold fitted cap. Then he hit DTLR and got some black Givenchy shorts and a black Givenchy polo where the collar was gold and the bottom half was gold. He topped it off with some gold Givenchy sneakers. He was in Macy's by the cologne when he heard his name.

"I know that ain't D'angelo Walker," Allison said.

"What's good, Allison?" Taz asked, giving her a hug

He hadn't seen her since his little sister's funeral. She was the one he used to get the loans from at the bank when he was investing in real estate.

"It's been a while."

"I know. How have you been?"

"Good, actually. I recently got promoted to regional manager so I supervise all the Wells Fargo's in the state."

"That's what's up! I know I can come get a million dollar loan now," Taz joked.

"I got you." She placed her hand on his chest, bringing back memories of when Taz had fucked her in her office on top of her desk. She was the second snowbunny he'd ever hit.

"You been doing your squats," Taz took her hand and spun her around, checking out her butt.

"Oh hush." She blushed "How long are you going to be in town?"

"A few days, then I'm leaving"

"You better call me so we can hook up before you leave." Allison ran her finger down the front of his shorts and walked away.

Taz left the mall and went to the African shop. He got a hot oil treatment and his dreads twisted. By the time he got done. It was eight o' clock. Taz went to his room to get ready to hit the club. He hopped in the shower, put on his outfit from the mall and a few dabs of Polo Red. He popped in the grill with his daughters' names across the front in pink and white diamonds. Then he completed the outfit with his black and white diamond chain and bracelet

"Where you at?" Taz called Slick.

"I'm about to leave the house right now," he whispered.

Confessions of a Gangsta 2

"Nigga, why is you whispering? I know you not sneaking out." He laughed.

"Fuck you!" Slick hung up.

Taz met Slick at Club Diamond. He hadn't been here since he'd first come home. They were deep as hell! Slick had brought the whole west side out and then when niggas heard Taz was home, all his south side niggas showed up. They were about a hundred deep all together. Taz hoped a nigga didn't get out of line because they were going to have a long night.

They entered the club without getting searched. *Somebody is going to fuck around and get killed in here*, Taz thought to himself. He could guarantee there were at least sixty guns in the club. Taz was going to chill for a little bit, then he was going to dip off and call Allison.

Taz was getting the celebrity treatment. Everywhere he turned, a nigga was dapping him up or a hoe was trying to get him to take them to a room.

"I told you, nigga! The city loves their own!" Slick yelled over the music.

Taz retired to the VIP section and tried to kick back, but there were hoes cutting up in there too.

"Feel this, daddy?" A chick came to him and put his hand under her dress, showing him how wet she was. "And my sister want to fuck too." She pointed to another girl across the room.

"Maybe next time, ma." He wiped her juices on her dress.

Taz could tell he was getting older because the club wasn't appealing to him like that anymore. Taz kicked it with his nigga for a few hours, but it was time to cut out, plus he'd had too many drinks. And he had Allison's pretty ass on his mind.

"Yo, I'm going to check y'all later." Taz got up and dapped as many niggas up as he could before he stumbled out

191

the door. "Damn, I drank too much," Taz said, getting in the rental

Taz put his gun on his lap and pulled out. He called Allison and got directions to her house. Taz was sitting at the stop light where Skibs Road and Marqanton Road intersect when a truck slammed into him from behind, knocking his gun to the floor. Taz was about to blank! He had reached down between his legs to grab the gun when a van pulled up beside him and esse's started piling out. Taz got ahold of the gun as they reached for his door handle. Taz started shooting through the door, hitting two of them before they returned his shots. They hit him in the leg, arm, and chest, which knocked his gun out of his hand. They snatched the door open and pulled Taz out of the car onto the pavement.

Taz knew this was the end of the road and he embraced it, but instead, one of them hit him with the butt of their AK, knocking him out.

Chapter 29

Taz woke up in a dark room strapped to a table. Taz lifted his head up and saw a camera pointed towards the table.

"Ha!" Taz laughed out loud. He knew exactly what the camera was for. He'd done the same thing with Javier. It was funny how things come back full circle.

"You seem to find your situation amusing. Why?" Hector stepped out of the shadows.

"Ah, the pussy finally comes out of hiding," Taz said.

"I have to give it to you, Taz, you have major cojones. You know the only reason you lived so long was because of my daughter. You know how many times I could've had you killed?"

"Kill me and get it over with, border hopper, and stop wolfing me. I lived so long because of me!" Taz amped.

"Lies!" Hector pounded the table. "Let me bring you back to earth. The night you were at Hooters with the dark-skinned chick, I could've snatch you. When you went to that basket-ball game in New York. The first time you met that meatball Vinnie at Primo's Pizza. The day the girl with the red dreads had your son and the time you rode that horse into the woods. I've had your life in my hands for a while now. I just knew it was going to kill my daughter when you died," Hector said.

Taz couldn't say anything because at the times he'd just named, Taz couldn't remember seeing one esse.

"No need to think about it. I told you my resources were endless when we first met. You chose the wrong side. If you had stayed on my team, these resources would be getting ready to be yours. I'm about to leave everything to Bella. You two together could've conquered the world, but now we'll never know. I would do you the way you did poor Javier, but

I know Bella is going to want an open casket," he said, pressing the record button on the camera "No one disrespects the Mexican Cartel and gets away with it," he said and pulled a .38 from his waistband. "Any last words, Taz?"

"Yeah. Suck my dick!"

Hector put the gun to Taz's temple and pulled the trigger.

***

"Bella, what's wrong with you?" Meosha asked, answering the door, seeing her crying "Kiki, come here!" she yelled.

Meosha led Bella and Ares into the house and into the living room.

"What you out here yelling about?" Kiki asked and then she saw Bella and that she'd been crying "No, no!" Kiki yelled, running back into her bedroom. She hadn't talked to Taz in three days. At first she thought he was just mad because of her decision to run OTF, but the longer she went without hearing from him, the more she knew something wasn't right. She could feel it in her stomach. And now Bella was in her living room crying. There could only be one reason for her to be crying and that reason would be something happening to Taz.

"Kiki, you need to come see this," Meosha said.

Kiki walked back into the living room just as Meosha pressed play on the DVD player. "Oh God!" Kiki put her hand over her mouth.

On the screen, Taz was strapped to a table while Hector walked around him. Kiki ignored the words. She was focused on her road dog, her thug, her baby daddy, her best friend. Then she saw Hector shoot Taz in the head and her legs gave out. She fell to the ground and started crying. She couldn't believe Taz was dead! Who was going to help her raise her kids? Who was going to watch her back?

"This is all your fault! If you would have set your pussy-ass daddy up a long time ago, Taz would still be here! My mom would still be here! You didn't really love him - not the way I did!" Kiki snapped, out of her mind. "Now what?" Kiki started seeing red. "Hector killed Taz and gets to live happily ever after? Get out my shit! I don't want to see you or hear from you ever again! I hope you can live with the fact that you're the reason Taz is dead!"

Bella grabbed Ares up and left. She had to plan Taz's funeral and no matter what Kiki said or thought, she loved Taz more than she loved herself. She just couldn't bring herself to choose between her father and Taz, but now she wished she had.

***

Day of the funeral

"Bitch, what, you got the flu or something?" Kiki asked, standing in the door of the bathroom as Meosha threw up for the fourth time that morning.

"Probably something I ate," she said.

"Well, you need to get it together. I'm not trying to be late."

Kiki had been doing her best to hold things together, but it was like when Taz died, a piece of her died too. Then she was about to drop the twins, D'angelo and Damiyana. Her emotions were all over the place. She was bucking the trend of wearing black. She was wearing an all-white Gucci pants suit. She'd gotten Taz's face tattooed on her chest and she'd gotten his name in big letters across the front of her neck. They were back in Fayetteville to bury Taz, the only thing Bella had done

195

right, in Kiki's eyes. Taz wouldn't have wanted to be buried anywhere else but his hometown. Kiki knew the funeral was going to be out of this world. It was going to be like they were burying the president.

"You need to bring your ass on!" Kiki yelled.

"I'm coming!" Meosha said, rinsing her mouth out. She'd been throwing up every morning for the last week. She looked down at the pregnancy test again and shook her head. She'd only fucked Taz one time and had gotten pregnant. She had to get an abortion. Kiki would lose her mind if she found out Meosha had Taz's child in her stomach, so she was going to keep this to herself. She walked down the steps in her black Valentino dress and saw Kiki waiting on her.

"Took your ass long enough," Kiki said and Meosha rolled her eyes.

They walked outside to a waiting Cadillac limo that Kiki had personally bought. Since taking over OTF, Kiki had made drastic changes to the organization, including the bulletproof limo. Kiki had upped security for all the higher-ups. Initially, OTF stood for only the family because all the main people were related by blood, but Kiki had learned that blood didn't make you family. She'd added people to the fold that weren't family, but were truly loyal. And she'd put Meosha in charge of the investigation firm.

Kiki had branched out from just Atlanta. OTF now had spots in Miami, Fayetteville, Memphis, and Baltimore. Within the next year, Kiki planned to expand to every major city on the east coast, then she was going to start moving west. She wanted to have OTF run the underworld in the U.S. She was going to make sure Taz's kids didn't have a care in the world and didn't have to resort to the street life.

They pulled up to Good Hope Baptist church and couldn't find a parking spot. There were cars lined up all the way down the road and there was still cars coming.

"Park at the door," Kiki told the dude driving the car.

Everyone waiting to get inside the church looked to see who was about to get out of the stretch Caddy. Kiki was quite the spectacle exiting the car in her white pantsuit. Her six and a half month stomach looked like she was ready to pop. Everyone moved as she and Meosha walked into the church. All eyes were on them as they made their way to the front and sat down.

Bella and Ares were across the aisle in the front row. Bella kept looking at Kiki, but Kiki wouldn't so much as bat an eye her way. Kiki turned to look around the church, taking in all the faces. She spotted a lot of familiar faces, but they had to go. Kiki got the attention of one of the OTF people scattered throughout the church and motioned her eyes towards Mary and gave them the sign she had to go.

"Y'all got me fucked up!" Mary yelled as they told her she had to go. "I knew him before half of the motherfuckers in here!" She started making a scene.

Kiki had heard enough. She got up and walked to the section where Mary was.

"I don't know what you came over here for! You not about to make me leave either, bitch!" Mary continued.

Kiki smirked and said, "Stop fronting! You didn't love Taz! You the same bitch that tried to set him up to get killed! Remember, I'm the reason your son ain't dead, you ungrateful nut rag!"

Keishana walked over and tried to stop things before they got out of hand, but Kiki was too far gone. Kiki pulled a baby nine out her Gucci tote bag and put it under Mary's chin. "Say

one more word and we're going to make this a double funeral.
Now get your shit and get the fuck out"

Mary grabbed her things and walked out without saying
another word. Kiki walked up to the closed casket and looked
at Taz's picture. All the emotions she'd been holding in came
pouring out.

"Why did you leave me, Taz?" Kiki cried. "This ain't how
our story is supposed to end!" Kiki had so much to say, but
she had to regain her composure. She couldn't afford to show
any weaknesses in front of her team. She got herself together
and left. She wouldn't be able to hold it together knowing Taz
was laid up inside that casket.

But there was one face that had to go.

***

Six months later

Kiki was at the house in Atlanta. She'd moved into her
mother's house.

"Give Mommy some kisses." She kissed her twins. They
were three months old now and getting bigger by the day.
They looked nothing like Kiki. They were mini Taz's. Every
minute of free time she had, she spent with her babies.

"Kiki, we need to talk," Meosha said, walking into the
nursery

"Get you some practice while we do. D'angelo needs his
diaper changed." Kiki handed Meosha the baby.

Meosha was seven-and-a-half months pregnant. She
hadn't gotten an abortion like she had initially planned. She
couldn't bring herself to kill her baby.

"I got something to tell you," Meosha said while wiping
D'angelo.

"I'm listening."

"I'm carrying Taz's daughter."

"Why you take so long to tell me?" Kiki asked calmly.

"I was scared, but don't blame Taz. It wasn't his fault."

"I know. It's clear you didn't realize the relationship me and my baby had. He'd told me what happened a while ago. I was just waiting on you to tell me. I kind've figured that was his baby, but I wasn't sure."

"So you not mad?"

Kiki backhanded her. "I'm disappointed - not mad - but at you, not him. What're you going to name her?"

"D'Angel."

"Ms. Kiki, it's someone at the door for you," the nanny came and told her.

"Who is it?"

"She said her name was Bella."

Kiki cocked her .45. She was about to kill her. Kiki went to the front door and put the gun in Bella's face

"Hear me out, Kiki," Bella said, ignoring the gun in her face.

"Two minutes. And I see you moved on already." Kiki looked down at her swollen stomach.

"This Taz's baby. You're not going to invite me in?" Bella asked and Kiki just stood there. "Whatever. I'm going to get to it then. I think me and you should team up. If you haven't heard, you're looking at the new head of the Mexican Cartel. I took my father's spot. Me and you together, OTF and the Mexican Cartel, on the same side would be unstoppable! I have the purest coke and resources you'd never imagine. What couldn't we do?"

"Bella, your father is the reason my other half is dead! And you say you love Taz, but the man responsible for his death is living the good life! You fake as hell, and I'm going to enjoy putting your brains on my lawn." Kiki raised her gun again.

Bella waved her hand above her head and ten esse's started walking up to the front door.

"Do you think they're going to save you?" Kiki put the gun to Bella's forehead.

"I have something for you," Bella told Kiki, unfazed by the gun pointed at her head. She waved the esse's up to her and they handed Kiki a box and walked back to their cars

Kiki lifted the lid and a smile crept to her face "Oh bitch, you sick! But you did that!"

"I loved Taz more than life itself and still do. So remember that next time you decide to question my love for OUR baby daddy."

"Come here," Kiki said, hugging Bella "Mexican Cartel and OTF together equals world domination. Let the games begin!"

Kiki dropped the box and Hector's head rolled onto the grass.

To Be Continued…
Confessions of a Gangsta 3
Coming Soon

Submission Guideline

Submit the first three chapters of your completed manuscript to ldpsubmissions@gmail.com, subject line: Your book's title. The manuscript must be in a .doc file and sent as an attachment. Document should be in Times New Roman, double spaced and in size 12 font. Also, provide your synopsis and full contact information. If sending multiple submissions, they must each be in a separate email.

Have a story but no way to send it electronically? You can still submit to LDP/Ca$h Presents. Send in the first three chapters, written or typed, of your completed manuscript to:

LDP: Submissions Dept
Po Box 944
Stockbridge, Ga 30281

DO NOT send original manuscript. Must be a duplicate.

Provide your synopsis and a cover letter containing your full contact information.

Thanks for considering LDP and Ca$h Presents.

Coming Soon from Lock Down Publications/Ca$h Presents

BOW DOWN TO MY GANGSTA

By **Ca$h**

TORN BETWEEN TWO

By **Coffee**

THE STREETS STAINED MY SOUL **II**

By **Marcellus Allen**

BLOOD OF A BOSS **VI**

SHADOWS OF THE GAME II

By **Askari**

LOYAL TO THE GAME **IV**

By **T.J. & Jelissa**

IF LOVING YOU IS WRONG... **III**

By **Jelissa**

TRUE SAVAGE **VII**

MIDNIGHT CARTEL III

DOPE BOY MAGIC IV

CITY OF KINGZ II

By **Chris Green**

BLAST FOR ME **III**

A SAVAGE DOPEBOY III

CUTTHROAT MAFIA III

By **Ghost**

A HUSTLER'S DECEIT III

KILL ZONE **II**

BAE BELONGS TO ME III

A DOPE BOY'S QUEEN III

By **Aryanna**

COKE KINGS V

KING OF THE TRAP II

By **T.J. Edwards**

GORILLAZ IN THE BAY V

3X KRAZY II

De'Kari

THE STREETS ARE CALLING II

Duquie Wilson

KINGPIN KILLAZ IV

STREET KINGS III

PAID IN BLOOD III

CARTEL KILLAZ IV

DOPE GODS III

Hood Rich

SINS OF A HUSTLA II

ASAD

KINGZ OF THE GAME VI

Playa Ray

SLAUGHTER GANG IV

RUTHLESS HEART IV

By **Willie Slaughter**

THE HEART OF A SAVAGE III

By **Jibril Williams**

FUK SHYT II

By **Blakk Diamond**

THE REALEST KILLAZ III

By Tranay Adams

TRAP GOD III

By Troublesome

YAYO IV

GHOST MOB

Stilloan Robinson

KINGPIN DREAMS III

By Paper Boi Rari

CREAM II

By Yolanda Moore

SON OF A DOPE FIEND III

By Renta

FOREVER GANGSTA II

GLOCKS ON SATIN SHEETS III

By Adrian Dulan

LOYALTY AIN'T PROMISED III

By Keith Williams

THE PRICE YOU PAY FOR LOVE II

By Destiny Skai

CONFESSIONS OF A GANGSTA III

By Nicholas Lock

I'M NOTHING WITHOUT HIS LOVE II

SINS OF A THUG II

By Monet Dragun

LIFE OF A SAVAGE IV

A GANGSTA'S QUR'AN III

MURDA SEASON III

GANGLAND CARTEL II

By **Romell Tukes**

QUIET MONEY III

THUG LIFE II

By **Trai'Quan**

THE STREETS MADE ME III

By **Larry D. Wright**

THE ULTIMATE SACRIFICE VI

IF YOU CROSS ME ONCE II

ANGEL III

By **Anthony Fields**

FRIEND OR FOE III

By **Mimi**

SAVAGE STORMS II

By **Meesha**

BLOOD ON THE MONEY II

By J-Blunt

THE STREETS WILL NEVER CLOSE II

By K'ajji

NIGHTMARES OF A HUSTLA II

By King Dream

THE WIFEY I USED TO BE II

By Nicole Goosby

IN THE ARM OF HIS BOSS

By Jamila

Nicholas Lock

Available Now

RESTRAINING ORDER **I & II**

By **CA$H & Coffee**

LOVE KNOWS NO BOUNDARIES **I II & III**

By **Coffee**

RAISED AS A GOON I, II, III & IV

BRED BY THE SLUMS I, II, III

BLAST FOR ME I & II

ROTTEN TO THE CORE I II III

A BRONX TALE I, II, III

DUFFEL BAG CARTEL I II III IV

HEARTLESS GOON I II III IV

A SAVAGE DOPEBOY I II

HEARTLESS GOON I II III

DRUG LORDS I II III

CUTTHROAT MAFIA I II

By **Ghost**

LAY IT DOWN **I & II**

LAST OF A DYING BREED

BLOOD STAINS OF A SHOTTA I & II III

By **Jamaica**

LOYAL TO THE GAME I II III

LIFE OF SIN I, II III

By **TJ & Jelissa**

BLOODY COMMAS I & II

SKI MASK CARTEL I II & III

KING OF NEW YORK I II,III IV V

RISE TO POWER I II III

COKE KINGS I II III IV

BORN HEARTLESS I II III IV

KING OF THE TRAP

By **T.J. Edwards**

IF LOVING HIM IS WRONG…I & II

LOVE ME EVEN WHEN IT HURTS I II III

By **Jelissa**

WHEN THE STREETS CLAP BACK I & II III

THE HEART OF A SAVAGE I II

By **Jibril Williams**

A DISTINGUISHED THUG STOLE MY HEART I II & III

LOVE SHOULDN'T HURT I II III IV

RENEGADE BOYS I II III IV

PAID IN KARMA I II III

SAVAGE STORMS

By **Meesha**

A GANGSTER'S CODE I &, II III

A GANGSTER'S SYN I II III

THE SAVAGE LIFE I II III

CHAINED TO THE STREETS I II III

BLOOD ON THE MONEY

By **J-Blunt**

PUSH IT TO THE LIMIT

By **Bre' Hayes**

BLOOD OF A BOSS **I, II, III, IV, V**

Nicholas Lock

SHADOWS OF THE GAME
By **Askari**
THE STREETS BLEED MURDER **I, II & III**
THE HEART OF A GANGSTA I II& III
By **Jerry Jackson**
CUM FOR ME I II III IV V VI
An **LDP Erotica Collaboration**
BRIDE OF A HUSTLA **I II & II**
THE FETTI GIRLS **I, II& III**
CORRUPTED BY A GANGSTA I, II III, IV
BLINDED BY HIS LOVE
THE PRICE YOU PAY FOR LOVE
DOPE GIRL MAGIC I II III
By **Destiny Skai**
WHEN A GOOD GIRL GOES BAD
By **Adrienne**
THE COST OF LOYALTY I II III
By Kweli
A GANGSTER'S REVENGE **I II III & IV**
THE BOSS MAN'S DAUGHTERS I II III IV V
A SAVAGE LOVE **I & II**
BAE BELONGS TO ME I II
A HUSTLER'S DECEIT I, II, III
WHAT BAD BITCHES DO I, II, III
SOUL OF A MONSTER I II III
KILL ZONE
A DOPE BOY'S QUEEN I II

By **Aryanna**

A KINGPIN'S AMBITON

A KINGPIN'S AMBITION **II**

I MURDER FOR THE DOUGH

By **Ambitious**

TRUE SAVAGE I II III IV V VI

DOPE BOY MAGIC I, II, III

MIDNIGHT CARTEL I II

CITY OF KINGZ

By **Chris Green**

A DOPEBOY'S PRAYER

By **Eddie "Wolf" Lee**

THE KING CARTEL **I, II & III**

By **Frank Gresham**

THESE NIGGAS AIN'T LOYAL **I, II & III**

By **Nikki Tee**

GANGSTA SHYT **I II &III**

By **CATO**

THE ULTIMATE BETRAYAL

By **Phoenix**

BOSS'N UP **I , II & III**

By **Royal Nicole**

I LOVE YOU TO DEATH

By Destiny J

I RIDE FOR MY HITTA

I STILL RIDE FOR MY HITTA

By **Misty Holt**

Nicholas Lock

LOVE & CHASIN' PAPER

By **Qay Crockett**

TO DIE IN VAIN

SINS OF A HUSTLA

By **ASAD**

BROOKLYN HUSTLAZ

By **Boogsy Morina**

BROOKLYN ON LOCK I & II

By **Sonovia**

GANGSTA CITY

By **Teddy Duke**

A DRUG KING AND HIS DIAMOND I & II III

A DOPEMAN'S RICHES

HER MAN, MINE'S TOO I, II

CASH MONEY HO'S

THE WIFEY I USED TO BE

By Nicole Goosby

TRAPHOUSE KING **I II & III**

KINGPIN KILLAZ I II III

STREET KINGS I II

PAID IN BLOOD **I II**

CARTEL KILLAZ I II III

DOPE GODS I II

By **Hood Rich**

LIPSTICK KILLAH **I, II, III**

CRIME OF PASSION I II & III

FRIEND OR FOE I II

Confessions of a Gangsta 2

By **Mimi**

STEADY MOBBN' **I, II, III**

THE STREETS STAINED MY SOUL

By **Marcellus Allen**

WHO SHOT YA **I, II, III**

SON OF A DOPE FIEND I II

Renta

GORILLAZ IN THE BAY **I II III IV**

TEARS OF A GANGSTA I II

3X KRAZY

DE'KARI

TRIGGADALE I II III

Elijah R. Freeman

GOD BLESS THE TRAPPERS I, II, III

THESE SCANDALOUS STREETS I, II, III

FEAR MY GANGSTA I, II, III IV, V

THESE STREETS DON'T LOVE NOBODY I, II

BURY ME A G I, II, III, IV, V

A GANGSTA'S EMPIRE I, II, III, IV

THE DOPEMAN'S BODYGAURD I II

THE REALEST KILLAZ I II

Tranay Adams

THE STREETS ARE CALLING

Duquie Wilson

MARRIED TO A BOSS... I II III

By **Destiny Skai & Chris Green**

KINGZ OF THE GAME I II III IV V

Nicholas Lock

Playa Ray
SLAUGHTER GANG I II III
RUTHLESS HEART I II III
By Willie Slaughter
FUK SHYT
By Blakk Diamond
DON'T F#CK WITH MY HEART I II
By Linnea
ADDICTED TO THE DRAMA I II III
IN THE ARM OF HIS BOSS II
By Jamila
YAYO I II III
A SHOOTER'S AMBITION I II
By S. Allen
TRAP GOD I II
By Troublesome
FOREVER GANGSTA
GLOCKS ON SATIN SHEETS I II
By Adrian Dulan
TOE TAGZ I II III
By Ah'Million
KINGPIN DREAMS I II
By Paper Boi Rari
CONFESSIONS OF A GANGSTA I II
By Nicholas Lock
I'M NOTHING WITHOUT HIS LOVE
SINS OF A THUG

By Monet Dragun

CAUGHT UP IN THE LIFE I II III

By Robert Baptiste

NEW TO THE GAME I II III

By **Malik D. Rice**

LIFE OF A SAVAGE I II III

A GANGSTA'S QUR'AN I II

MURDA SEASON I II

GANGLAND CARTEL

By **Romell Tukes**

LOYALTY AIN'T PROMISED I II

By Keith Williams

QUIET MONEY I II

THUG LIFE

By **Trai'Quan**

THE STREETS MADE ME I II

By **Larry D. Wright**

THE ULTIMATE SACRIFICE I, II, III, IV, V

KHADIFI

IF YOU CROSS ME ONCE

ANGEL I II

By **Anthony Fields**

THE LIFE OF A HOOD STAR

By Ca\$h & Rashia Wilson

THE STREETS WILL NEVER CLOSE

By K'ajji

CREAM

Nicholas Lock

By Yolanda Moore
NIGHTMARES OF A HUSTLA
By King Dream

BOOKS BY LDP'S CEO, CA$H

TRUST IN NO MAN

TRUST IN NO MAN 2

TRUST IN NO MAN 3

BONDED BY BLOOD

SHORTY GOT A THUG

THUGS CRY

THUGS CRY 2

THUGS CRY 3

TRUST NO BITCH

TRUST NO BITCH 2

TRUST NO BITCH 3

TIL MY CASKET DROPS

RESTRAINING ORDER

RESTRAINING ORDER 2

IN LOVE WITH A CONVICT

LIFE OF A HOOD STAR

Nicholas Lock

www.ingramcontent.com/pod-product-compliance
Lightning Source LLC
Chambersburg PA
CBHW070457260626
47161CB00004B/1346